Mom

JURASSIC PARK
VOLUME 5

AFTERSHOCKS!

ADAPTED BY
STEVE ENGLEHART,
ARMANDO GIL
AND DELL BARRAS

Spotlight

IDW

visit us at www.abdopublishing.com

Reinforced library bound editions published in 2014 by Spotlight, a division of the ABDO Group, PO Box 398166, Minneapolis, Minnesota 55439. Published by agreement with IDW Publishing. www.idwpublishing.com

Printed in the United States of America, North Mankato, Minnesota.
052013
092013
This book contains at least 10% recycled materials.

Library of Congress Cataloging-in-Publication Data

Englehart, Steve.
Jurassic Park / adapted by Steve Englehart, Armand Gil, and Dell Barras. -- Reinforced library edition.
pages cm. -- (Jurassic Park ; v. 5-10)
Summary: "Three days after their escape from Isla Nublar, Dr. Alan Grant and Dr. Ellie Sattler have returned to help confine the dinosaurs. When the escaped raptors remain elusive, Grant and Sattler go on their own mission... and discover they aren't the only ones looking for raptors!"-- Provided by publisher.
ISBN 978-1-61479-187-4 (vol. 5: Aftershocks!) -- ISBN 978-1-61479-188-1 (vol. 6: Dark cargo!) -- ISBN 978-1-61479-189-8 (vol. 7: Raptors attack) -- ISBN 978-1-61479-190-4 (vol. 8: Animals vs. men) -- ISBN 978-1-61479-191-1 (vol. 9: Animals vs. gods!) -- ISBN 978-1-61479-192-8 (vol. 10: Gods vs. men!)
1. Graphic novels. [1. Graphic novels. 2. Dinosaurs--Fiction. 3. Science fiction.] I. Gil, Armand. II. Barras, Dell. III. Title.
PZ7.7.E6Jur 2013
741.5'973--dc23

2013013372

Spotlight

All Spotlight books are reinforced library binding and manufactured in the United States of America.

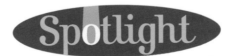

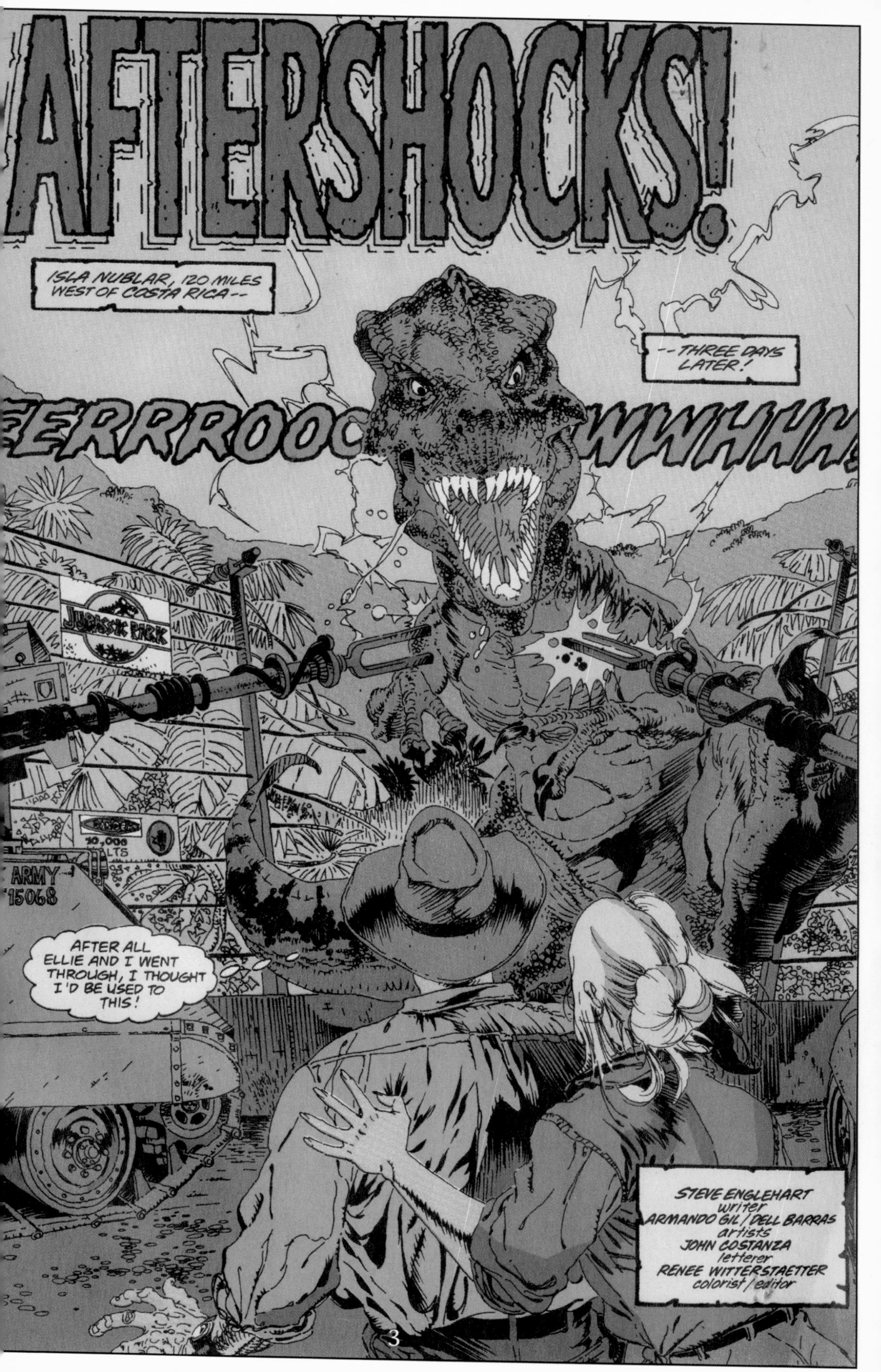

AFTERSHOCKS!
ISLA NUBLAR, 120 MILES WEST OF COSTA RICA--
--THREE DAYS LATER!
ERRROOOWWHHH
JURASSIC PARK
ARMY 15068
AFTER ALL ELLIE AND I WENT THROUGH, I THOUGHT I'D BE USED TO THIS!
STEVE ENGLEHART writer
ARMANDO GIL / DELL BARRAS artists
JOHN COSTANZA letterer
RENEE WITTERSTAETTER colorist / editor

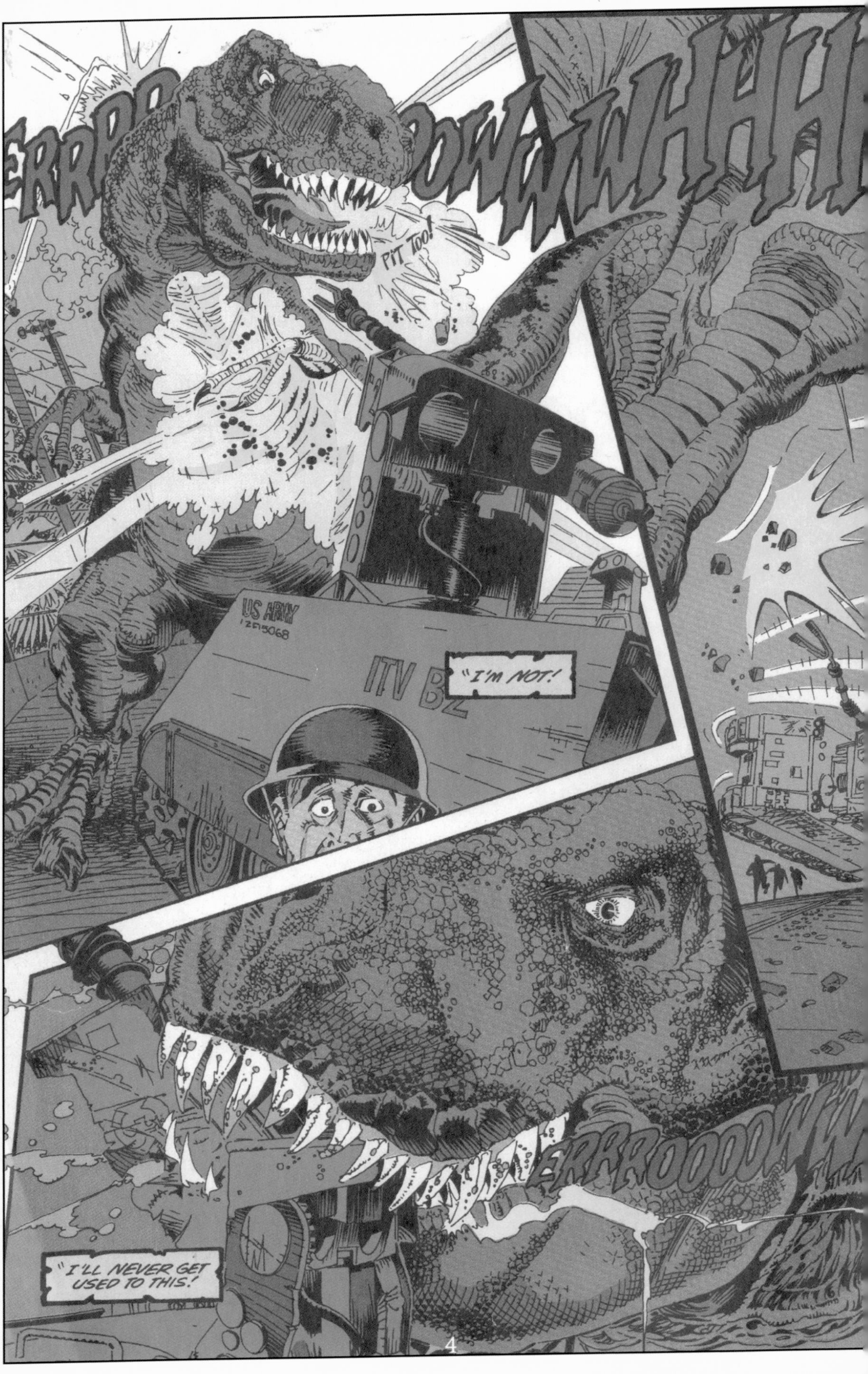
ERRROOWWWHHHH
PIT TOO!
US ARMY
12F15068
ITV B2
"I'M NOT!
ERRROOOOOWW
"I'LL NEVER GET USED TO THIS!

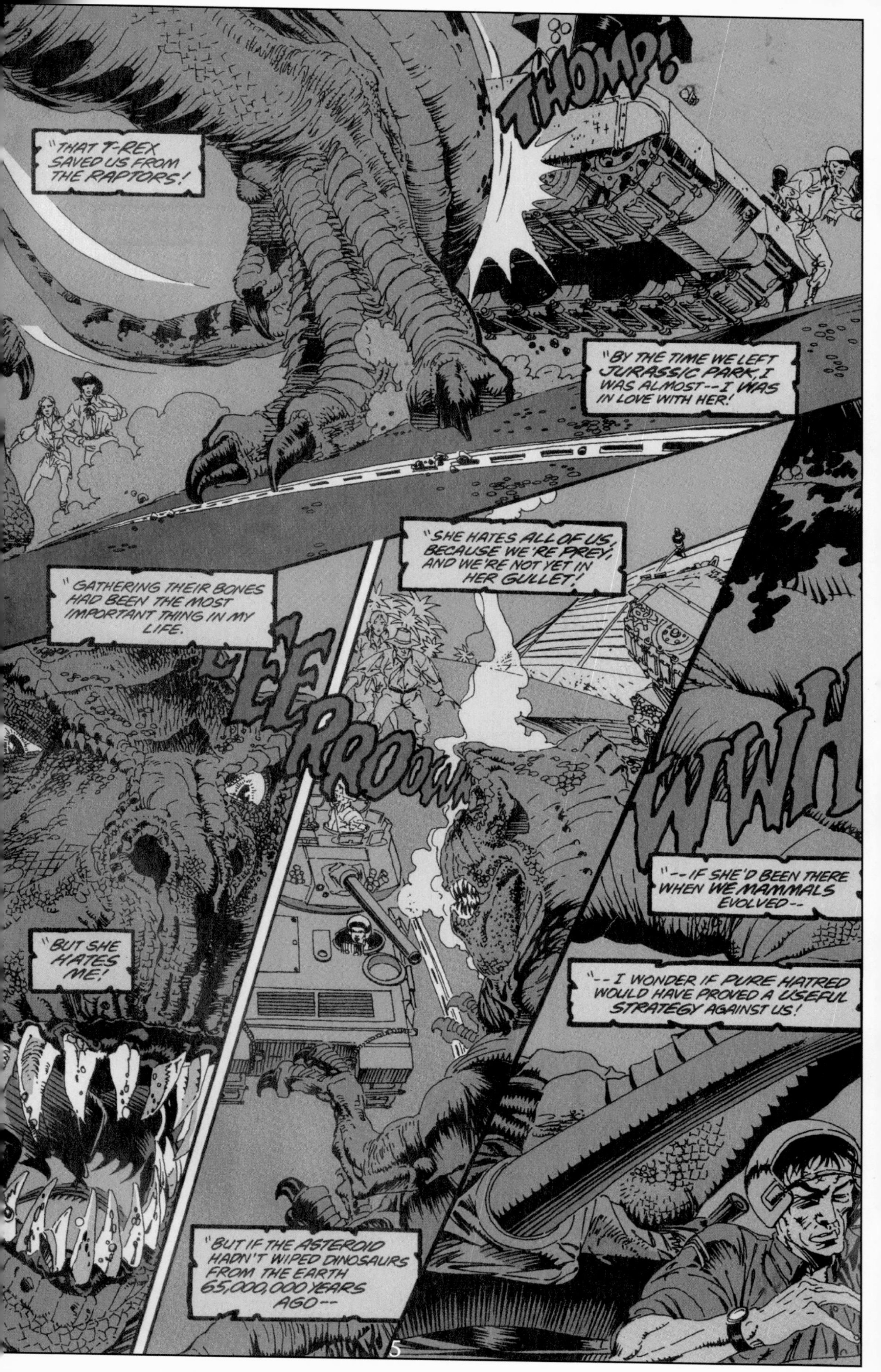
THOMP!
"THAT T-REX SAVED US FROM THE RAPTORS!
"BY THE TIME WE LEFT JURASSIC PARK, I WAS ALMOST--I WAS IN LOVE WITH HER!
"GATHERING THEIR BONES HAD BEEN THE MOST IMPORTANT THING IN MY LIFE.
"BUT SHE HATES ME!
"SHE HATES ALL OF US, BECAUSE WE'RE PREY, AND WE'RE NOT YET IN HER GULLET!
EEERROOOWW
"BUT IF THE ASTEROID HADN'T WIPED DINOSAURS FROM THE EARTH 65,000,000 YEARS AGO--
"--IF SHE'D BEEN THERE WHEN WE MAMMALS EVOLVED--
"--I WONDER IF PURE HATRED WOULD HAVE PROVED A USEFUL STRATEGY AGAINST US!
WWH

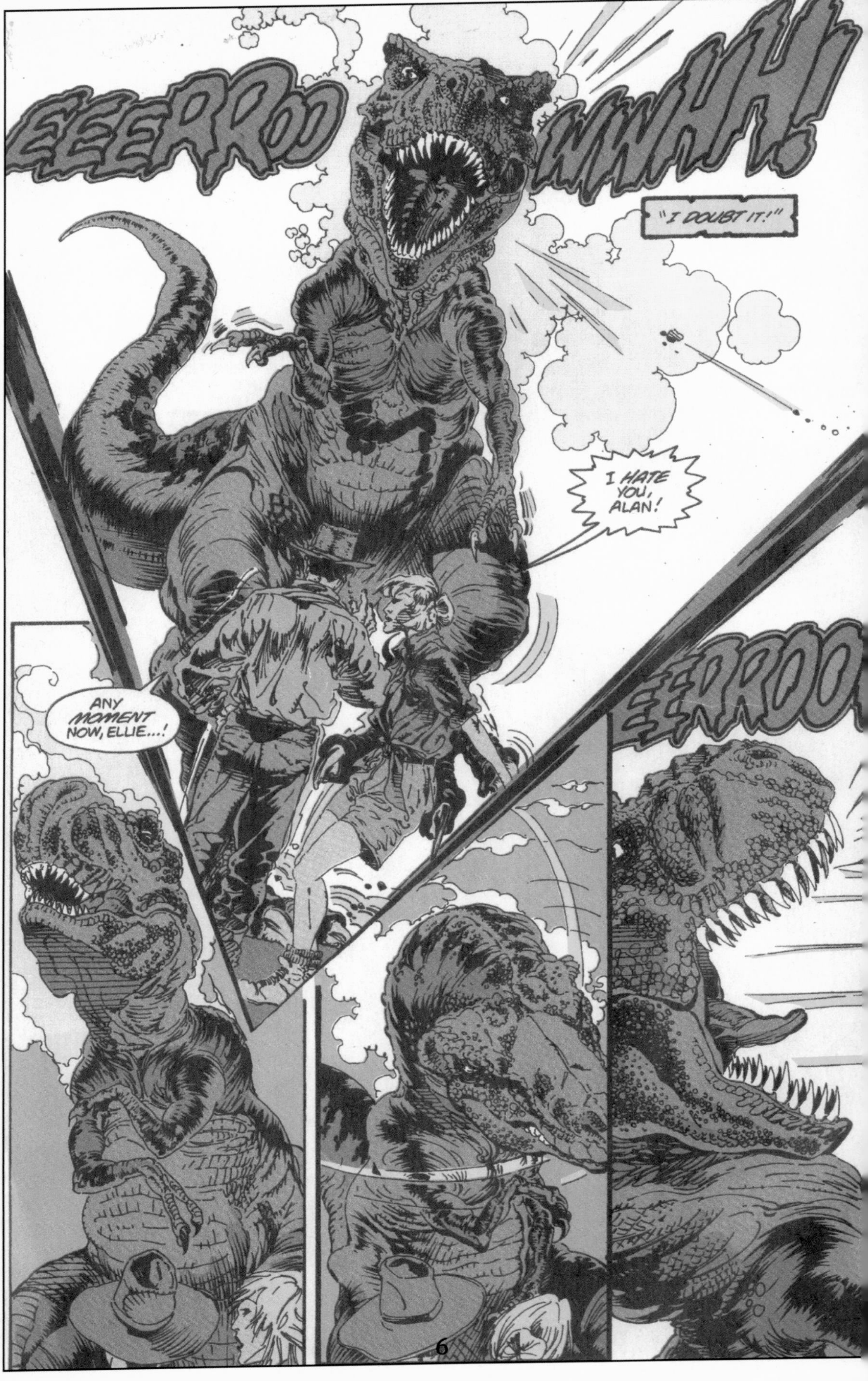
EEEERROOO WWAAH!
"I DOUBT IT!"
I HATE YOU, ALAN!
ANY MOMENT NOW, ELLIE...!
EERROO

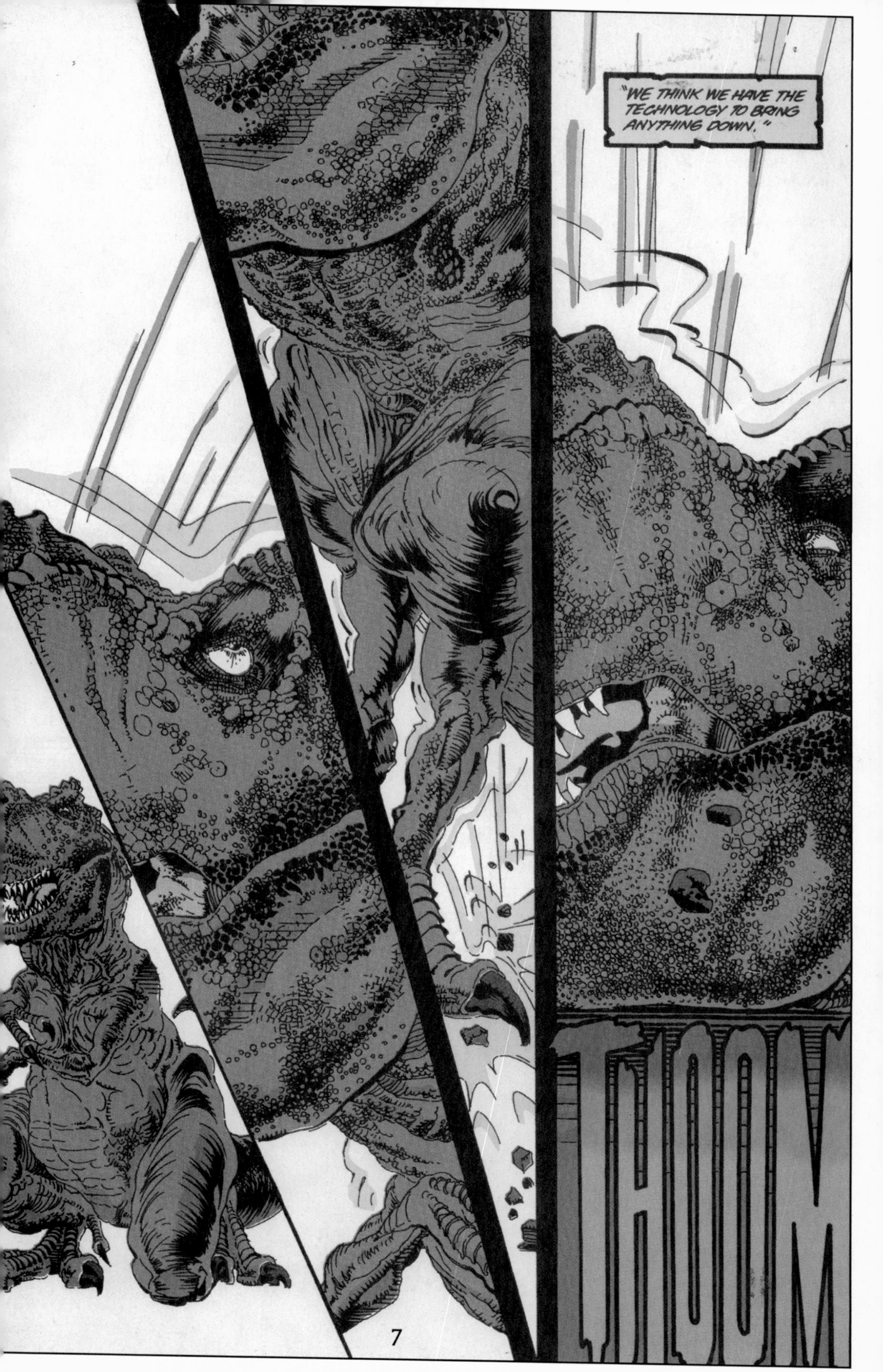
"WE THINK WE HAVE THE TECHNOLOGY TO BRING ANYTHING DOWN."
THOOM

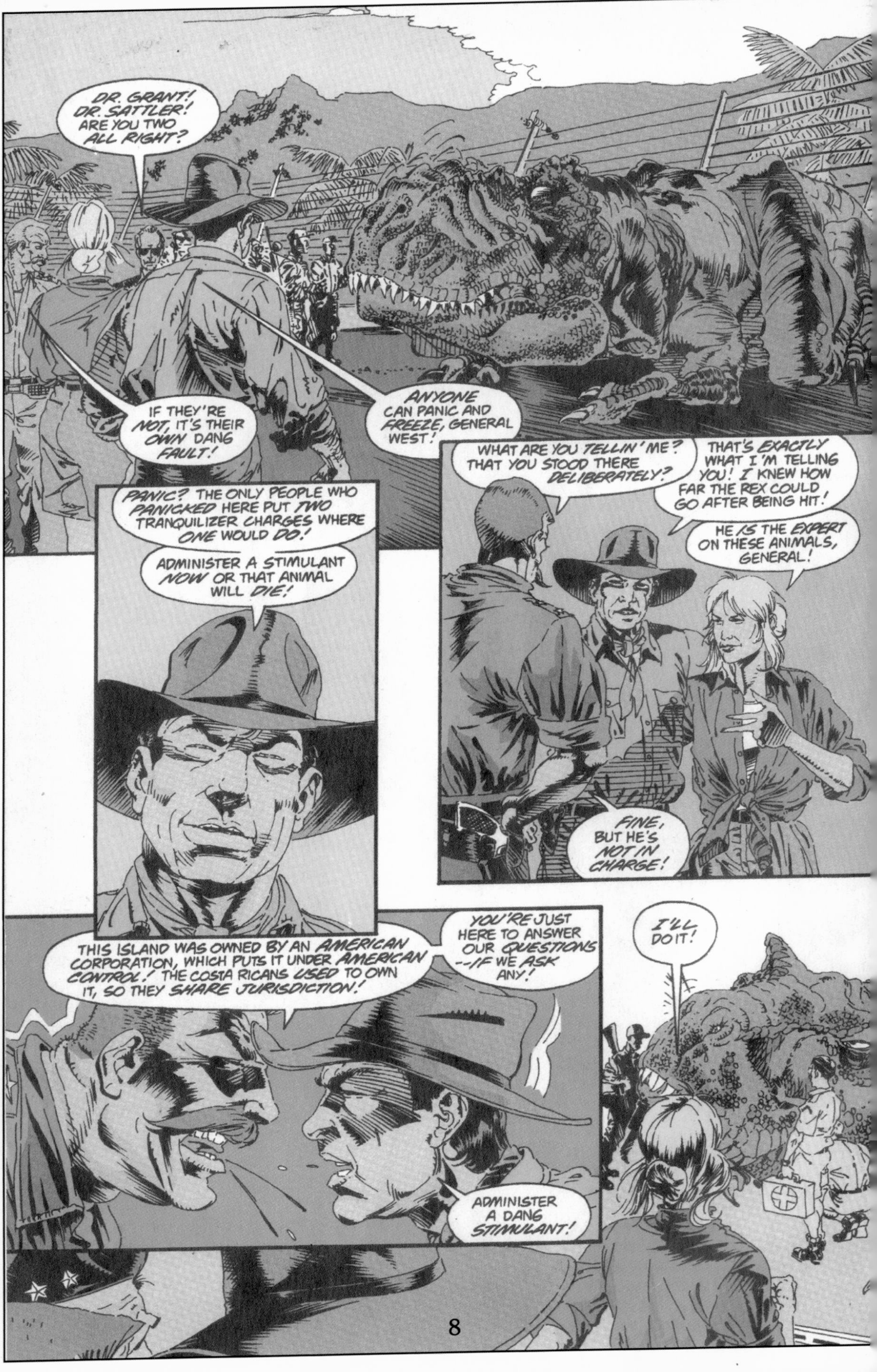
DR. GRANT! DR. SATTLER! ARE YOU TWO ALL RIGHT?
IF THEY'RE NOT, IT'S THEIR OWN DANG FAULT!
ANYONE CAN PANIC AND FREEZE, GENERAL WEST!
PANIC? THE ONLY PEOPLE WHO PANICKED HERE PUT TWO TRANQUILIZER CHARGES WHERE ONE WOULD DO!
ADMINISTER A STIMULANT NOW OR THAT ANIMAL WILL DIE!
WHAT ARE YOU TELLIN' ME? THAT YOU STOOD THERE DELIBERATELY?
THAT'S EXACTLY WHAT I'M TELLING YOU! I KNEW HOW FAR THE REX COULD GO AFTER BEING HIT!
HE IS THE EXPERT ON THESE ANIMALS, GENERAL!
FINE, BUT HE'S NOT IN CHARGE!
THIS ISLAND WAS OWNED BY AN AMERICAN CORPORATION, WHICH PUTS IT UNDER AMERICAN CONTROL! THE COSTA RICANS USED TO OWN IT, SO THEY SHARE JURISDICTION!
YOU'RE JUST HERE TO ANSWER OUR QUESTIONS --IF WE ASK ANY!
ADMINISTER A DANG STIMULANT!
I'LL DO IT!

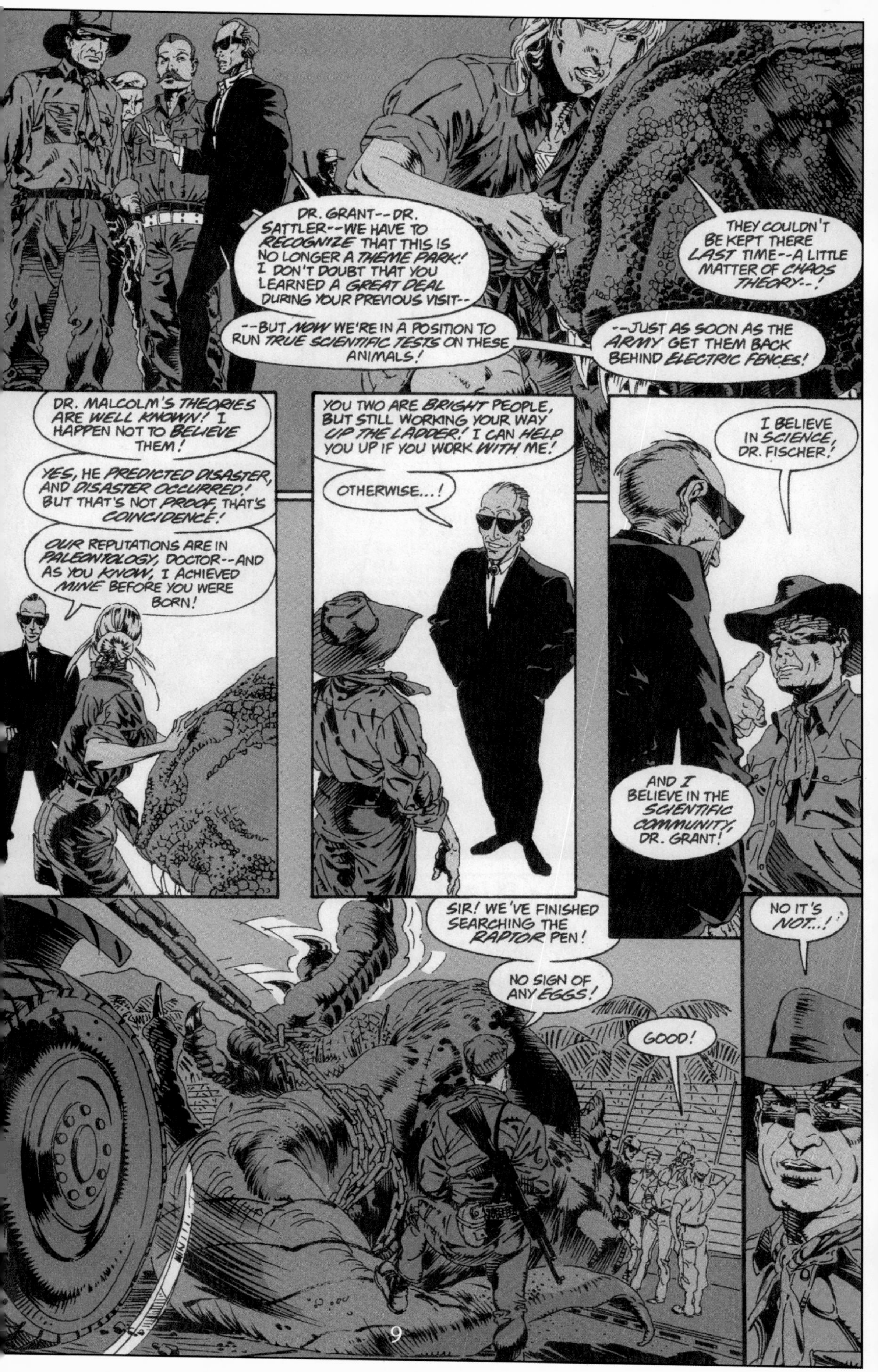
DR. GRANT--DR. SATTLER--WE HAVE TO RECOGNIZE THAT THIS IS NO LONGER A THEME PARK! I DON'T DOUBT THAT YOU LEARNED A GREAT DEAL DURING YOUR PREVIOUS VISIT--
--BUT NOW WE'RE IN A POSITION TO RUN TRUE SCIENTIFIC TESTS ON THESE ANIMALS!
--JUST AS SOON AS THE ARMY GET THEM BACK BEHIND ELECTRIC FENCES!
THEY COULDN'T BE KEPT THERE LAST TIME--A LITTLE MATTER OF CHAOS THEORY--!
DR. MALCOLM'S THEORIES ARE WELL KNOWN! I HAPPEN NOT TO BELIEVE THEM!
YES, HE PREDICTED DISASTER, AND DISASTER OCCURRED! BUT THAT'S NOT PROOF, THAT'S COINCIDENCE!
OUR REPUTATIONS ARE IN PALEONTOLOGY, DOCTOR--AND AS YOU KNOW, I ACHIEVED MINE BEFORE YOU WERE BORN!
YOU TWO ARE BRIGHT PEOPLE, BUT STILL WORKING YOUR WAY UP THE LADDER! I CAN HELP YOU UP IF YOU WORK WITH ME!
OTHERWISE...!
I BELIEVE IN SCIENCE, DR. FISCHER!
AND I BELIEVE IN THE SCIENTIFIC COMMUNITY, DR. GRANT!
SIR! WE'VE FINISHED SEARCHING THE RAPTOR PEN!
NO SIGN OF ANY EGGS!
GOOD!
NO IT'S NOT...!

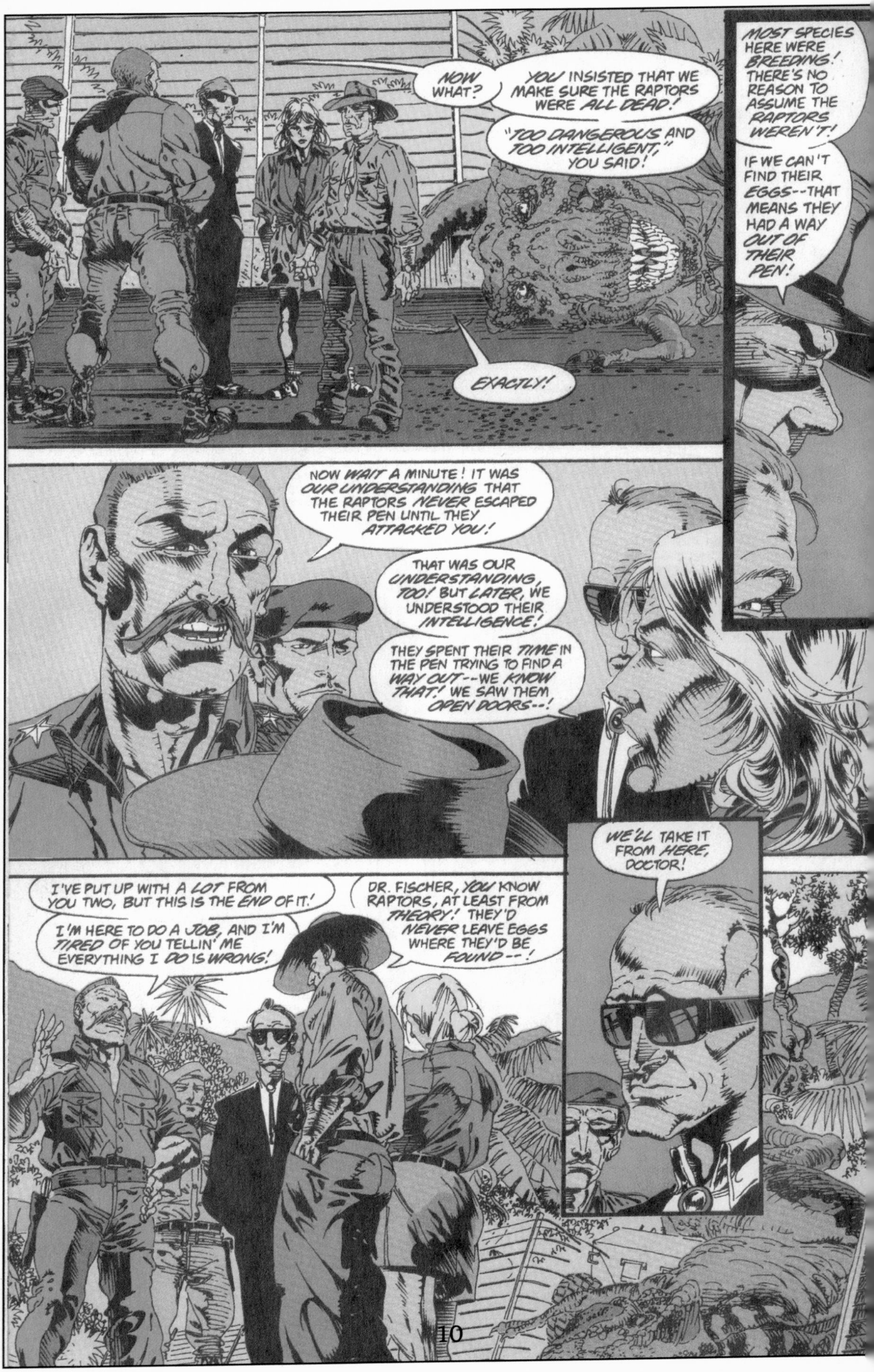
NOW WHAT?
YOU INSISTED THAT WE MAKE SURE THE RAPTORS WERE ALL DEAD!
"TOO DANGEROUS AND TOO INTELLIGENT," YOU SAID!
EXACTLY!
MOST SPECIES HERE WERE BREEDING! THERE'S NO REASON TO ASSUME THE RAPTORS WEREN'T!
IF WE CAN'T FIND THEIR EGGS--THAT MEANS THEY HAD A WAY OUT OF THEIR PEN!
NOW WAIT A MINUTE! IT WAS OUR UNDERSTANDING THAT THE RAPTORS NEVER ESCAPED THEIR PEN UNTIL THEY ATTACKED YOU!
THAT WAS OUR UNDERSTANDING, TOO! BUT LATER, WE UNDERSTOOD THEIR INTELLIGENCE!
THEY SPENT THEIR TIME IN THE PEN TRYING TO FIND A WAY OUT--WE KNOW THAT! WE SAW THEM OPEN DOORS--!
I'VE PUT UP WITH A LOT FROM YOU TWO, BUT THIS IS THE END OF IT!
I'M HERE TO DO A JOB, AND I'M TIRED OF YOU TELLIN' ME EVERYTHING I DO IS WRONG!
DR. FISCHER, YOU KNOW RAPTORS, AT LEAST FROM THEORY! THEY'D NEVER LEAVE EGGS WHERE THEY'D BE FOUND--!
WE'LL TAKE IT FROM HERE, DOCTOR!

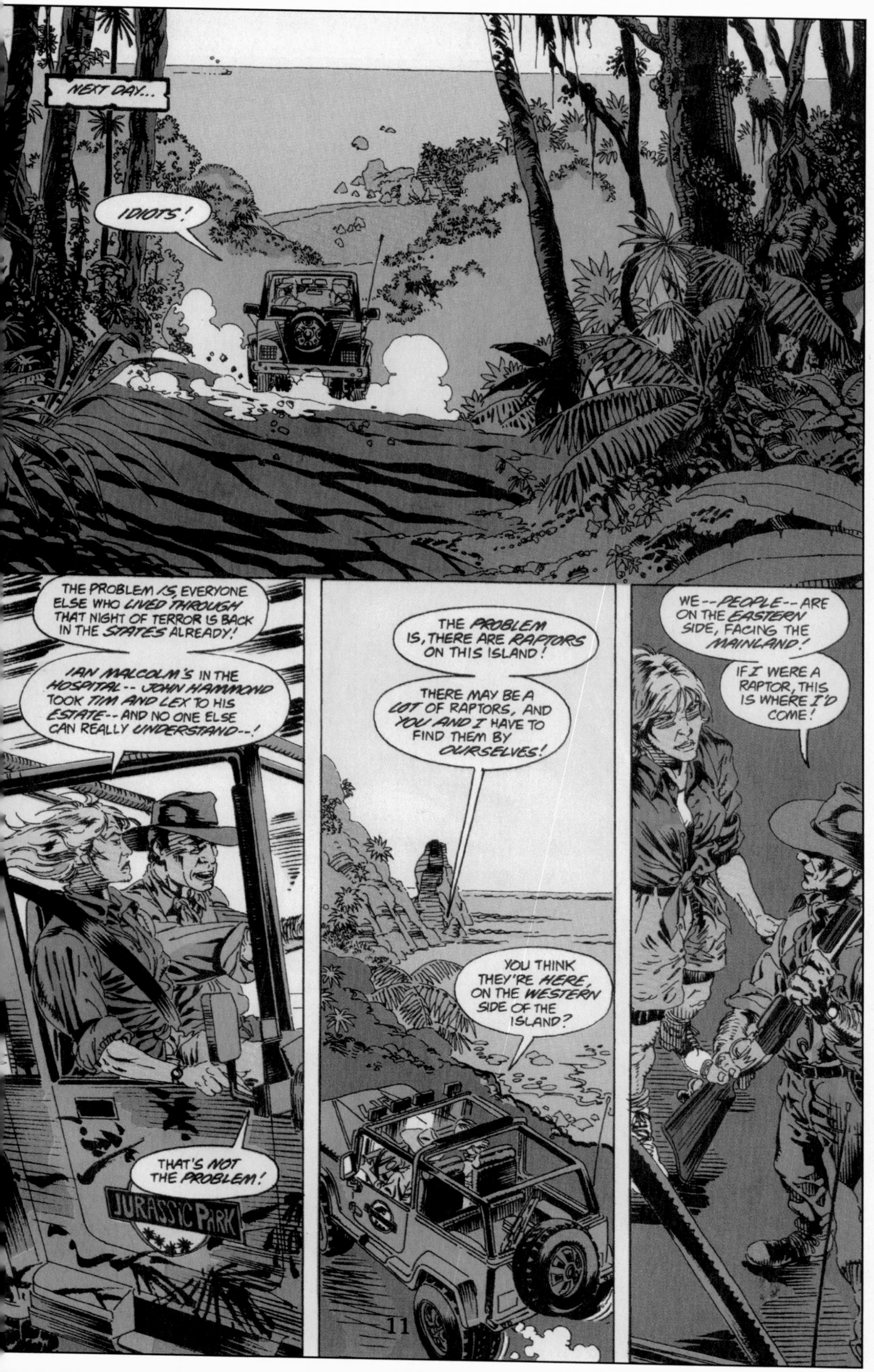
NEXT DAY...
IDIOTS!
THE PROBLEM IS, EVERYONE ELSE WHO LIVED THROUGH THAT NIGHT OF TERROR IS BACK IN THE STATES ALREADY!
IAN MALCOLM'S IN THE HOSPITAL-- JOHN HAMMOND TOOK TIM AND LEX TO HIS ESTATE-- AND NO ONE ELSE CAN REALLY UNDERSTAND--!
THAT'S NOT THE PROBLEM!
JURASSIC PARK
THE PROBLEM IS, THERE ARE RAPTORS ON THIS ISLAND!
THERE MAY BE A LOT OF RAPTORS, AND YOU AND I HAVE TO FIND THEM BY OURSELVES!
YOU THINK THEY'RE HERE, ON THE WESTERN SIDE OF THE ISLAND?
WE--PEOPLE--ARE ON THE EASTERN SIDE, FACING THE MAINLAND!
IF I WERE A RAPTOR, THIS IS WHERE I'D COME!

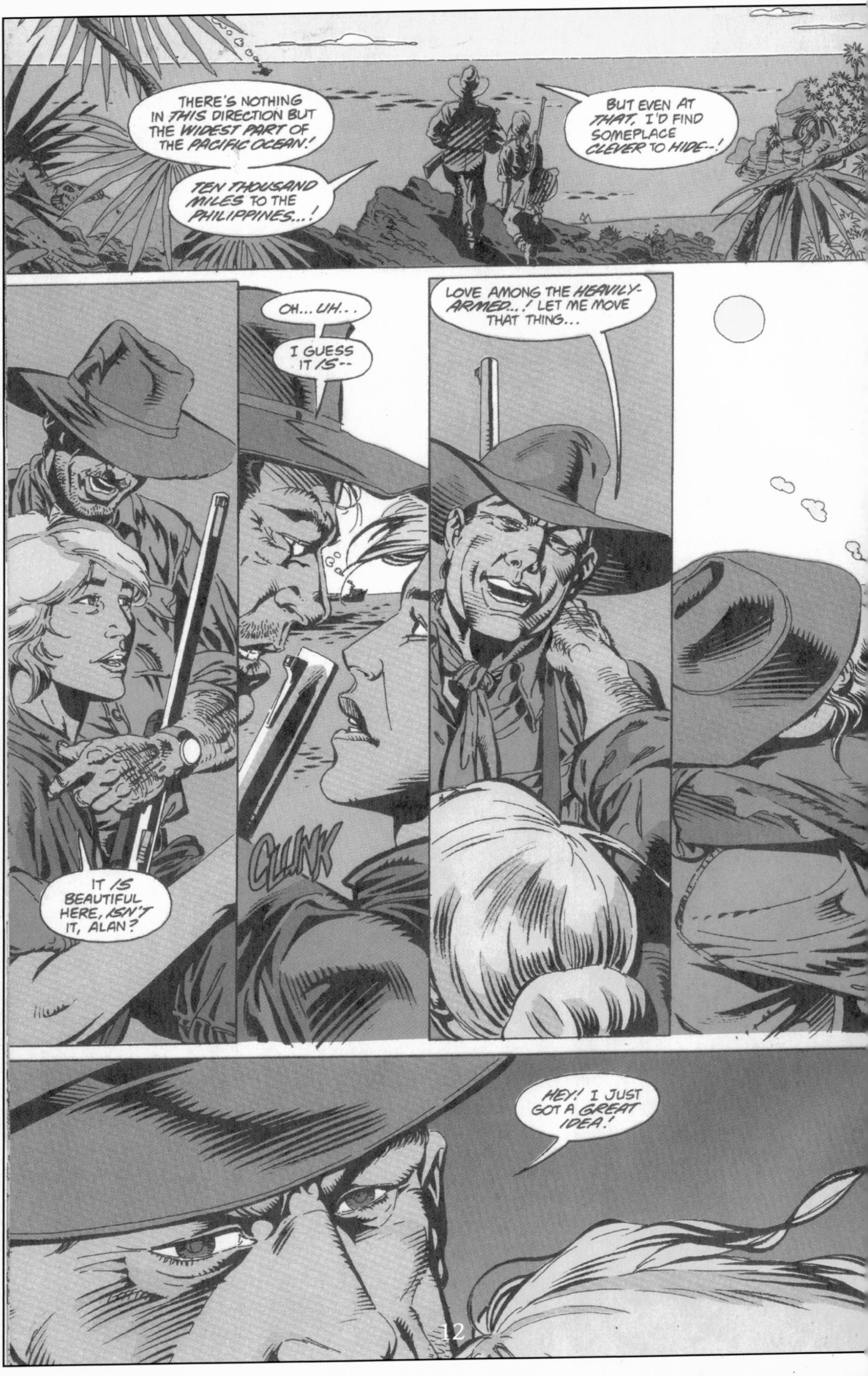
THERE'S NOTHING IN THIS DIRECTION BUT THE WIDEST PART OF THE PACIFIC OCEAN!
TEN THOUSAND MILES TO THE PHILIPPINES...!
BUT EVEN AT THAT, I'D FIND SOMEPLACE CLEVER TO HIDE--!
IT IS BEAUTIFUL HERE, ISN'T IT, ALAN?
OH... UH...
I GUESS IT IS--
CLUNK
LOVE AMONG THE HEAVILY-ARMED...! LET ME MOVE THAT THING...
HEY! I JUST GOT A GREAT IDEA!

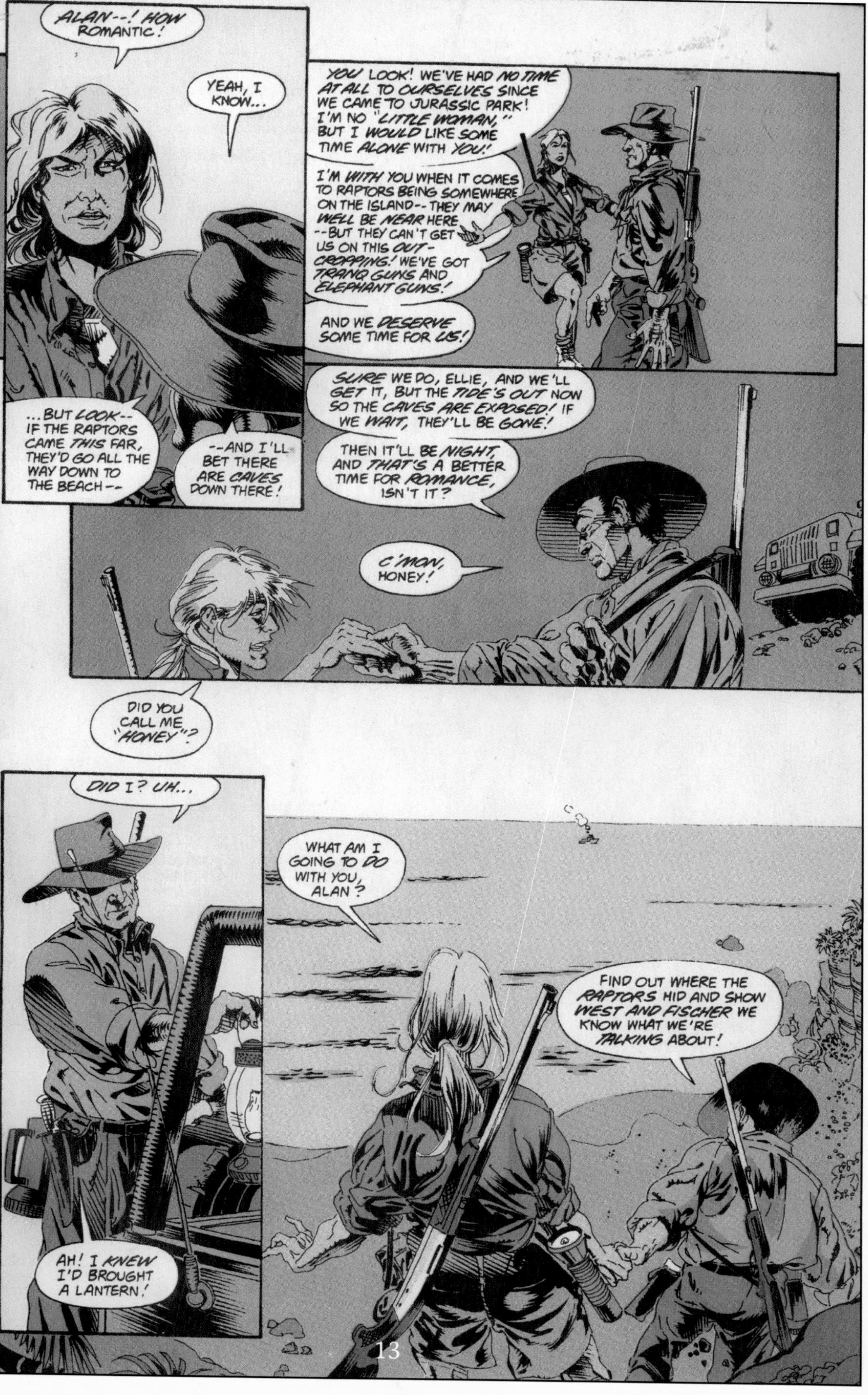
ALAN--! HOW ROMANTIC!
YEAH, I KNOW...
YOU LOOK! WE'VE HAD NO TIME AT ALL TO OURSELVES SINCE WE CAME TO JURASSIC PARK! I'M NO "LITTLE WOMAN," BUT I WOULD LIKE SOME TIME ALONE WITH YOU!
I'M WITH YOU WHEN IT COMES TO RAPTORS BEING SOMEWHERE ON THE ISLAND--THEY MAY WELL BE NEAR HERE --BUT THEY CAN'T GET US ON THIS OUT-CROPPING! WE'VE GOT TRANQ GUNS AND ELEPHANT GUNS!
AND WE DESERVE SOME TIME FOR US!
...BUT LOOK--IF THE RAPTORS CAME THIS FAR, THEY'D GO ALL THE WAY DOWN TO THE BEACH--
--AND I'LL BET THERE ARE CAVES DOWN THERE!
SURE WE DO, ELLIE, AND WE'LL GET IT, BUT THE TIDE'S OUT NOW SO THE CAVES ARE EXPOSED! IF WE WAIT, THEY'LL BE GONE!
THEN IT'LL BE NIGHT, AND THAT'S A BETTER TIME FOR ROMANCE, ISN'T IT?
C'MON, HONEY!
DID YOU CALL ME "HONEY"?
DID I? UH...
AH! I KNEW I'D BROUGHT A LANTERN!
WHAT AM I GOING TO DO WITH YOU, ALAN?
FIND OUT WHERE THE RAPTORS HID AND SHOW WEST AND FISCHER WE KNOW WHAT WE'RE TALKING ABOUT!

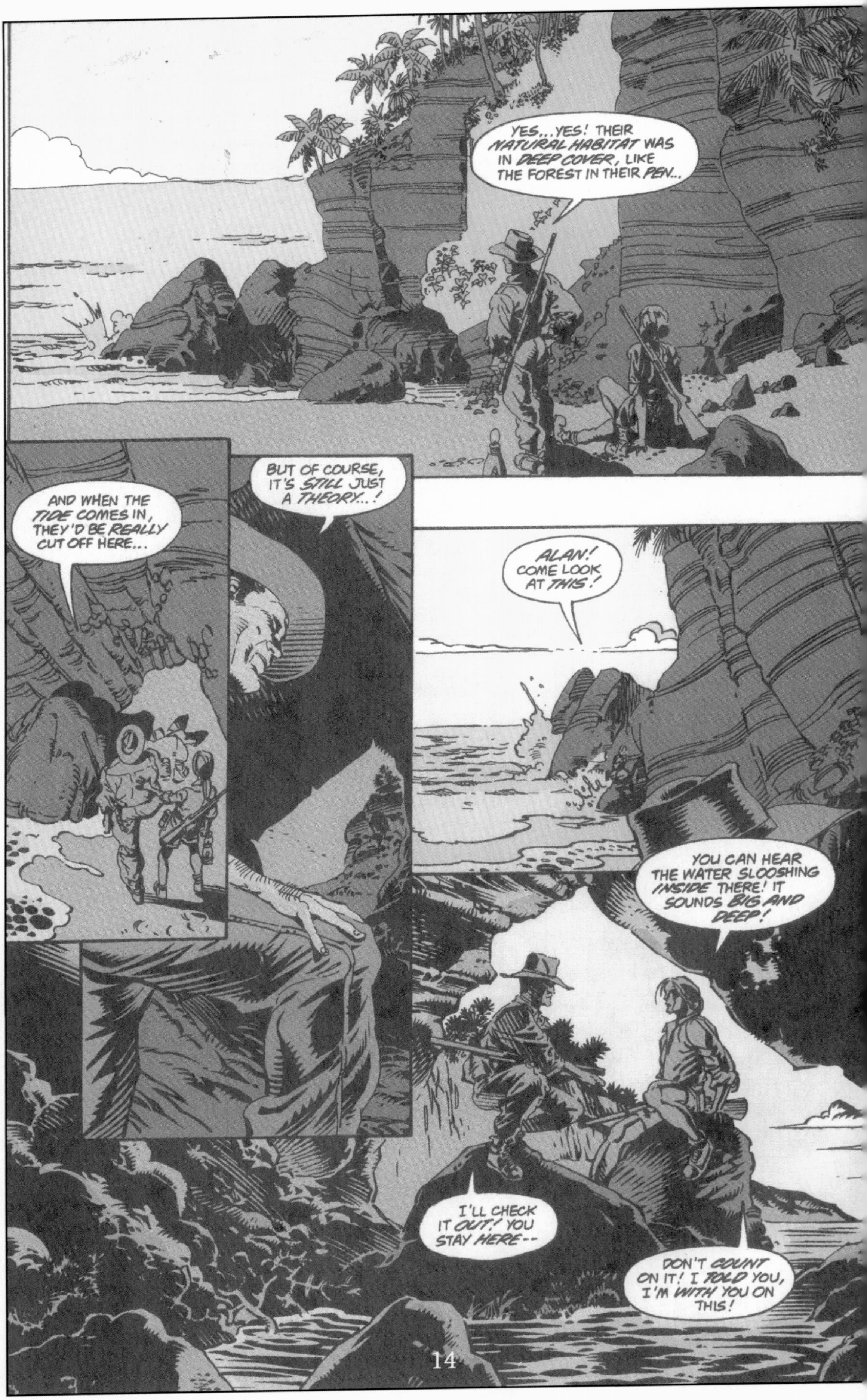
YES...YES! THEIR NATURAL HABITAT WAS IN DEEP COVER, LIKE THE FOREST IN THEIR PEN...
AND WHEN THE TIDE COMES IN, THEY'D BE REALLY CUT OFF HERE...
BUT OF COURSE, IT'S STILL JUST A THEORY...!
ALAN! COME LOOK AT THIS!
YOU CAN HEAR THE WATER SLOOSHING INSIDE THERE! IT SOUNDS BIG AND DEEP!
I'LL CHECK IT OUT! YOU STAY HERE--
DON'T COUNT ON IT! I TOLD YOU, I'M WITH YOU ON THIS!

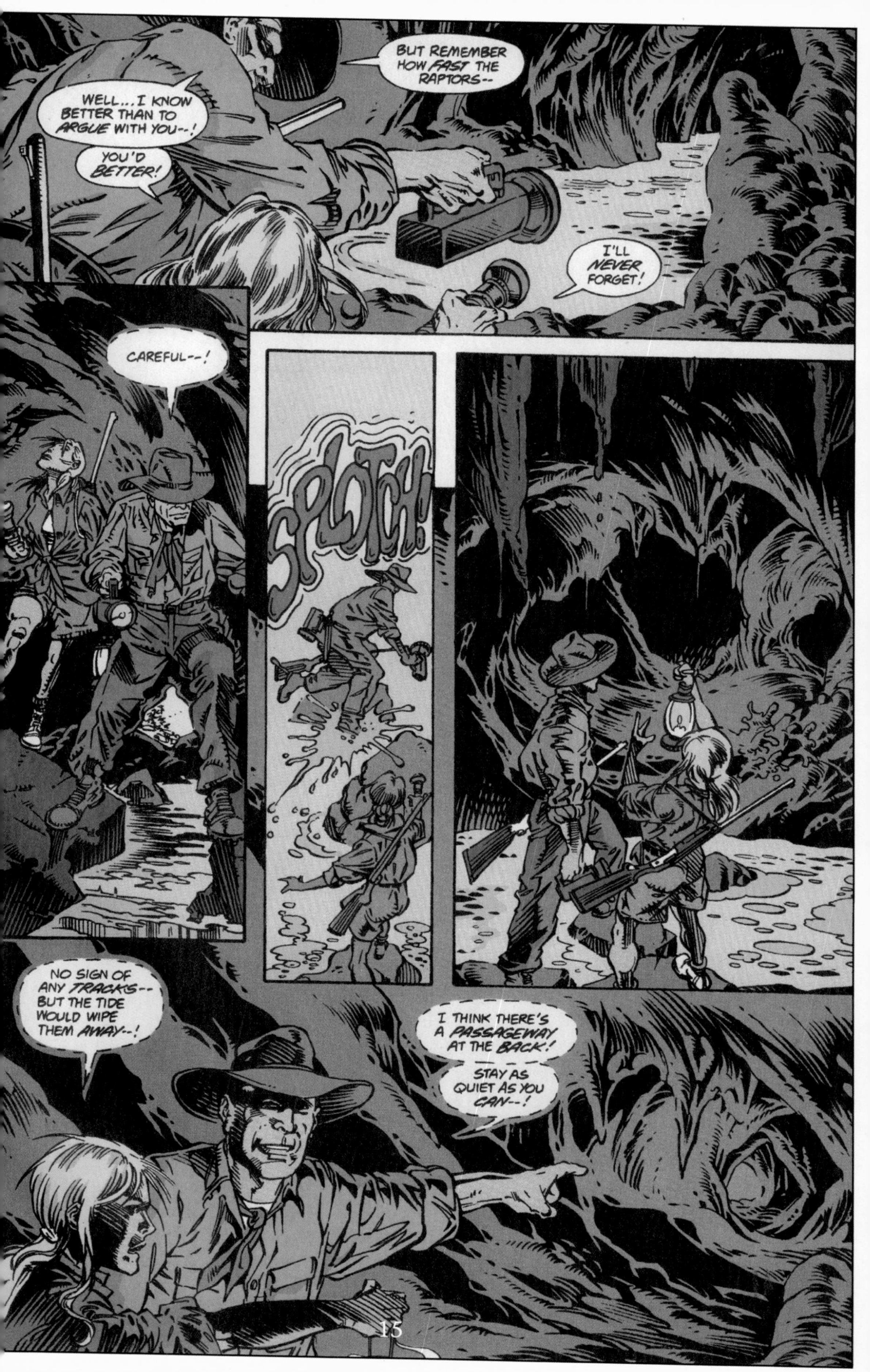
BUT REMEMBER HOW FAST THE RAPTORS--
WELL... I KNOW BETTER THAN TO ARGUE WITH YOU--!
YOU'D BETTER!
I'LL NEVER FORGET!
CAREFUL--!
SPLOTCH!
NO SIGN OF ANY TRACKS-- BUT THE TIDE WOULD WIPE THEM AWAY--!
I THINK THERE'S A PASSAGEWAY AT THE BACK!
STAY AS QUIET AS YOU CAN--!

WHAT THE --?!! ...

SHLLOOONK!

WHO ARE YOU?

GEORGE LAWALA! YOU MUST BE DOCTORS GRANT AND SATTLER!

BUT WHO ARE YOU?

THE TRUTH? I'M A HUNTER-- THE BEST THERE IS, TO TELL THE WHOLE TRUTH!

SOME PEOPLE KNOW ABOUT THE DINOSAURS ON THIS ISLAND, AND THEY HIRED ME TO BRING THEM SOME!

I'M CHARGING THEM A FORTUNE!

HOW'D YOU GET HERE?

RODE MY JET IN FROM A BOAT OFFSHORE! I CHOSE THIS SIDE OF THE ISLAND BECAUSE I THOUGHT EVERYONE WAS ON THE OTHER SIDE--

-- CHOSE THIS CAVE BECAUSE I WANTED COM- PLETE COVER!

BELIEVE ME, I'M AS SURPRISED TO FIND YOU HERE AS YOU ARE TO FIND ME!

BUT I'M TRAINED FOR THIS SORT OF WORK!

SHOOM

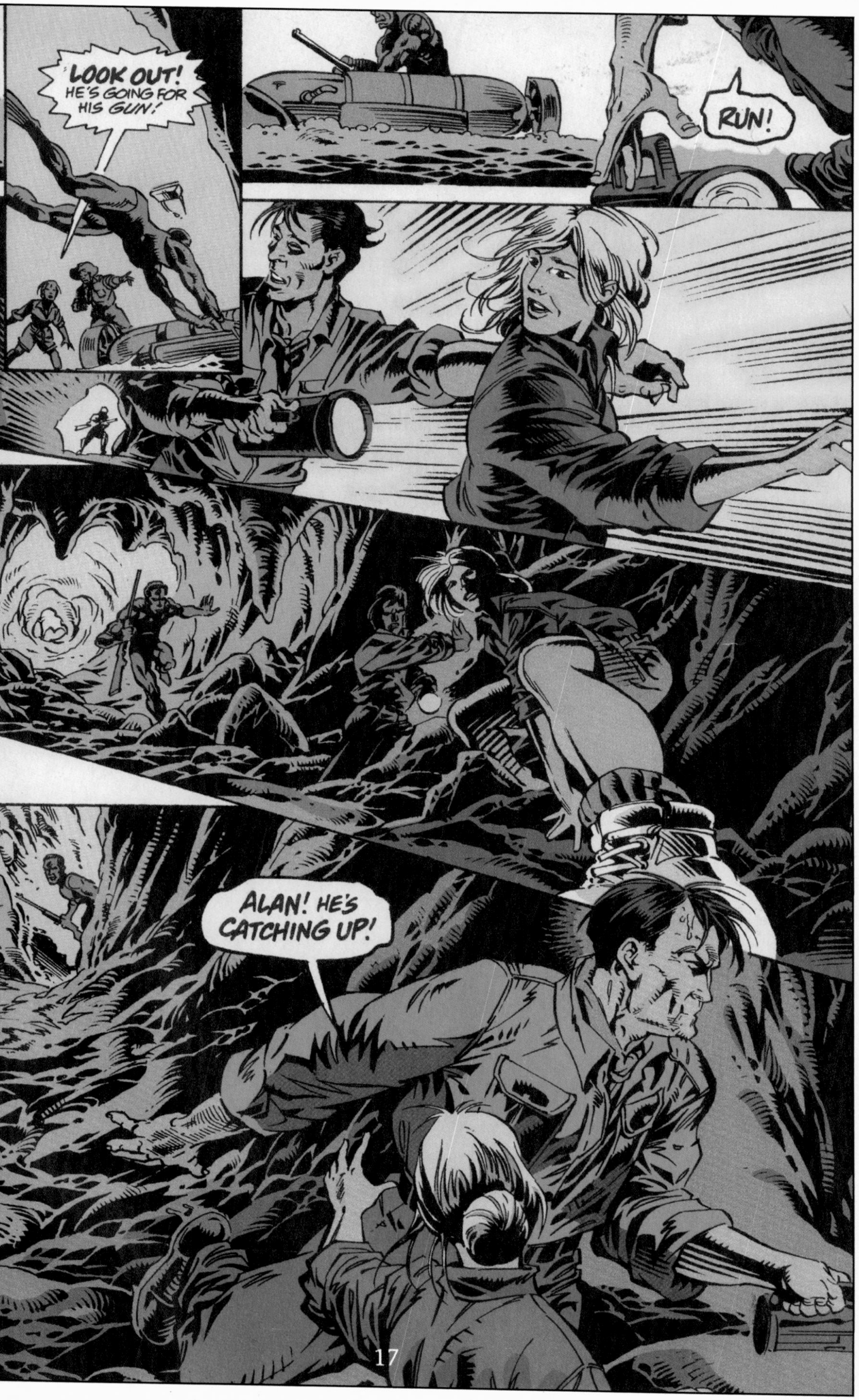
LOOK OUT! HE'S GOING FOR HIS GUN!
RUN!
ALAN! HE'S CATCHING UP!

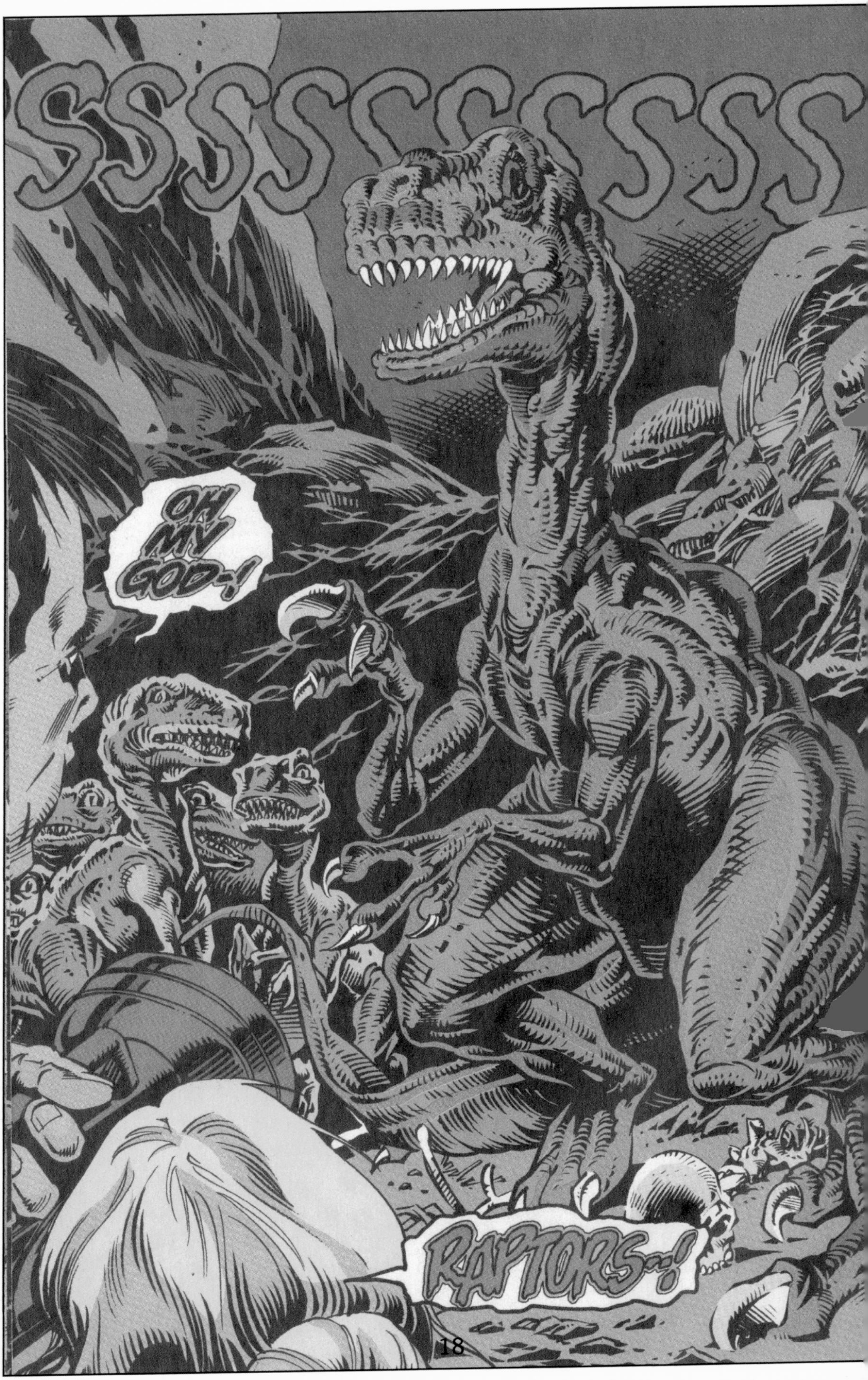
SSSSSSSSSSS
OH MY GOD--!
RAPTORS--!

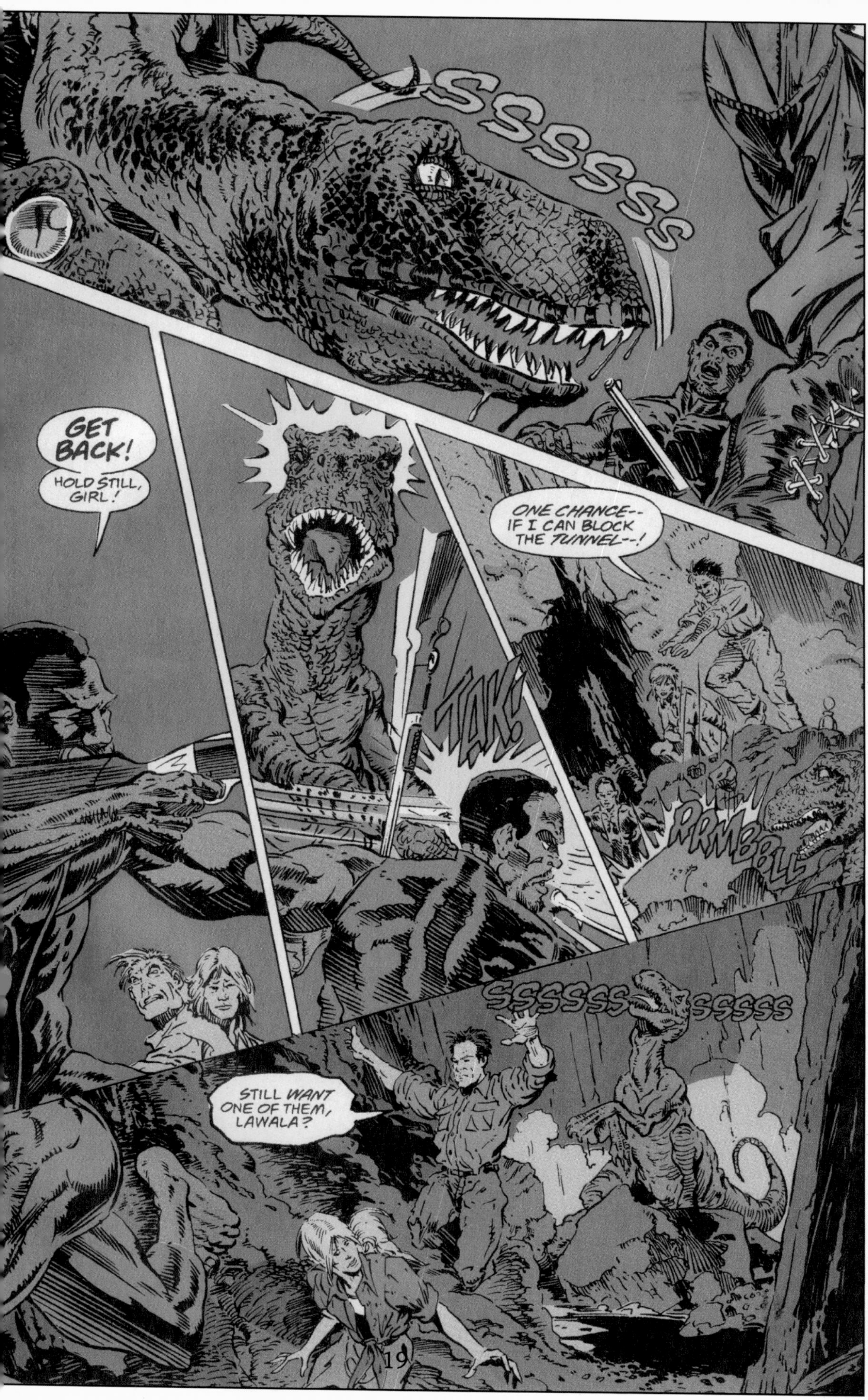
SSSSSS
GET BACK!
HOLD STILL, GIRL!
TAK!
ONE CHANCE-- IF I CAN BLOCK THE TUNNEL--!
RRMBBLL
SSSSSS SSSSS
STILL WANT ONE OF THEM, LAWALA?

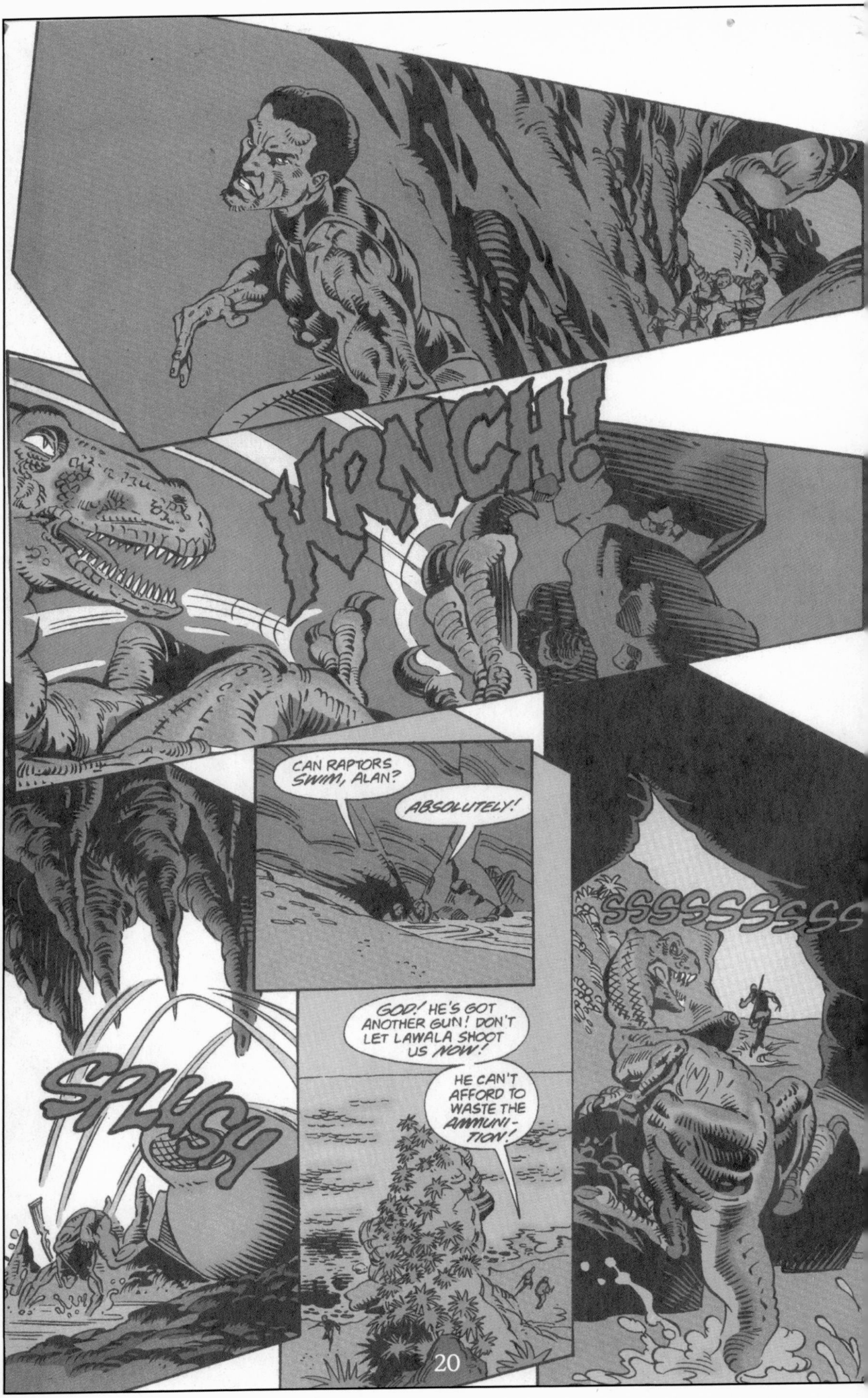
KRNCH!
CAN RAPTORS SWIM, ALAN?
ABSOLUTELY!
SSSSSSSSSS
SPLUSH
GOD! HE'S GOT ANOTHER GUN! DON'T LET LAWALA SHOOT US NOW!
HE CAN'T AFFORD TO WASTE THE AMMUNITION!

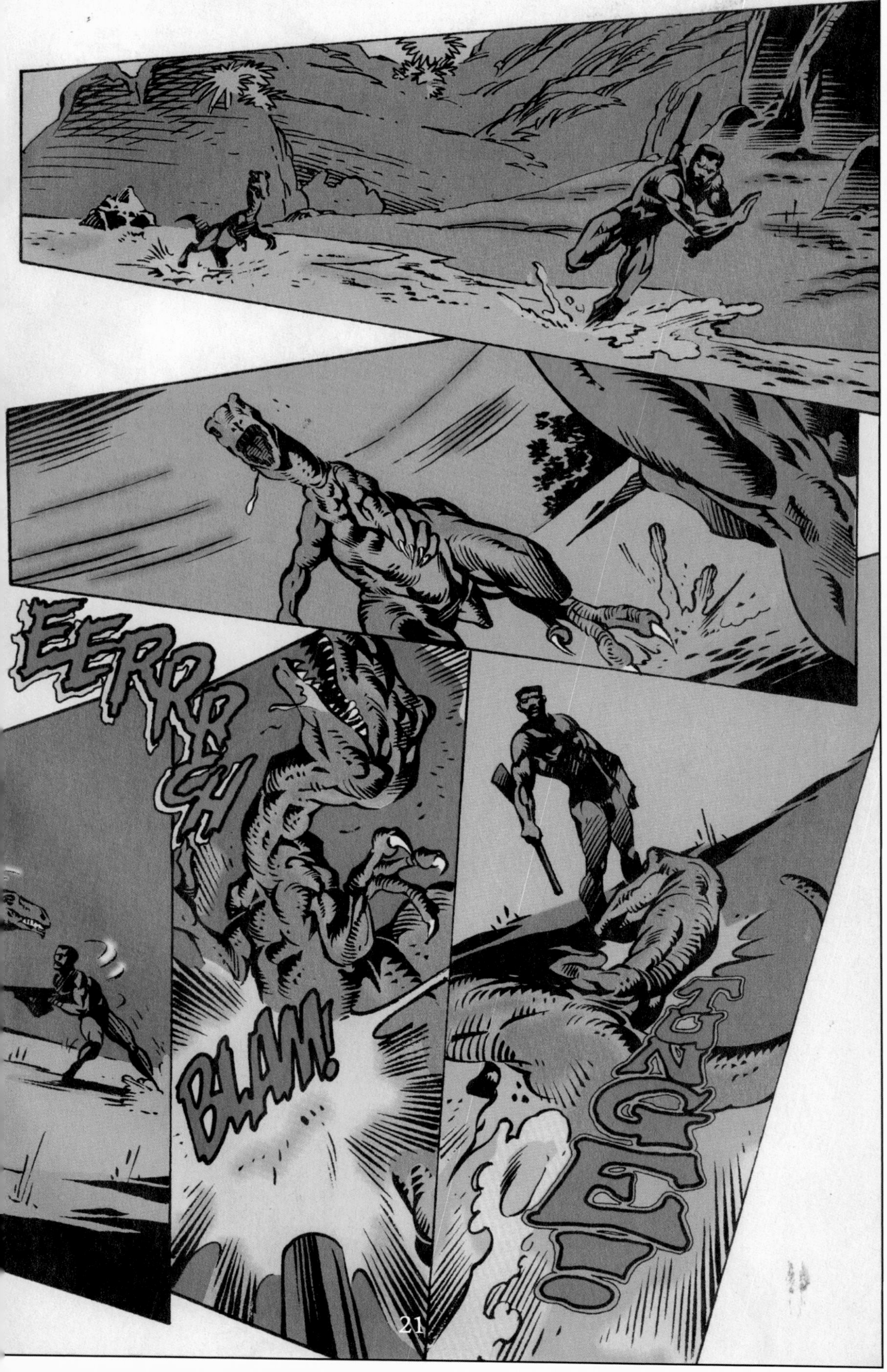
EERRRCH
BLAM!
EEEGGH

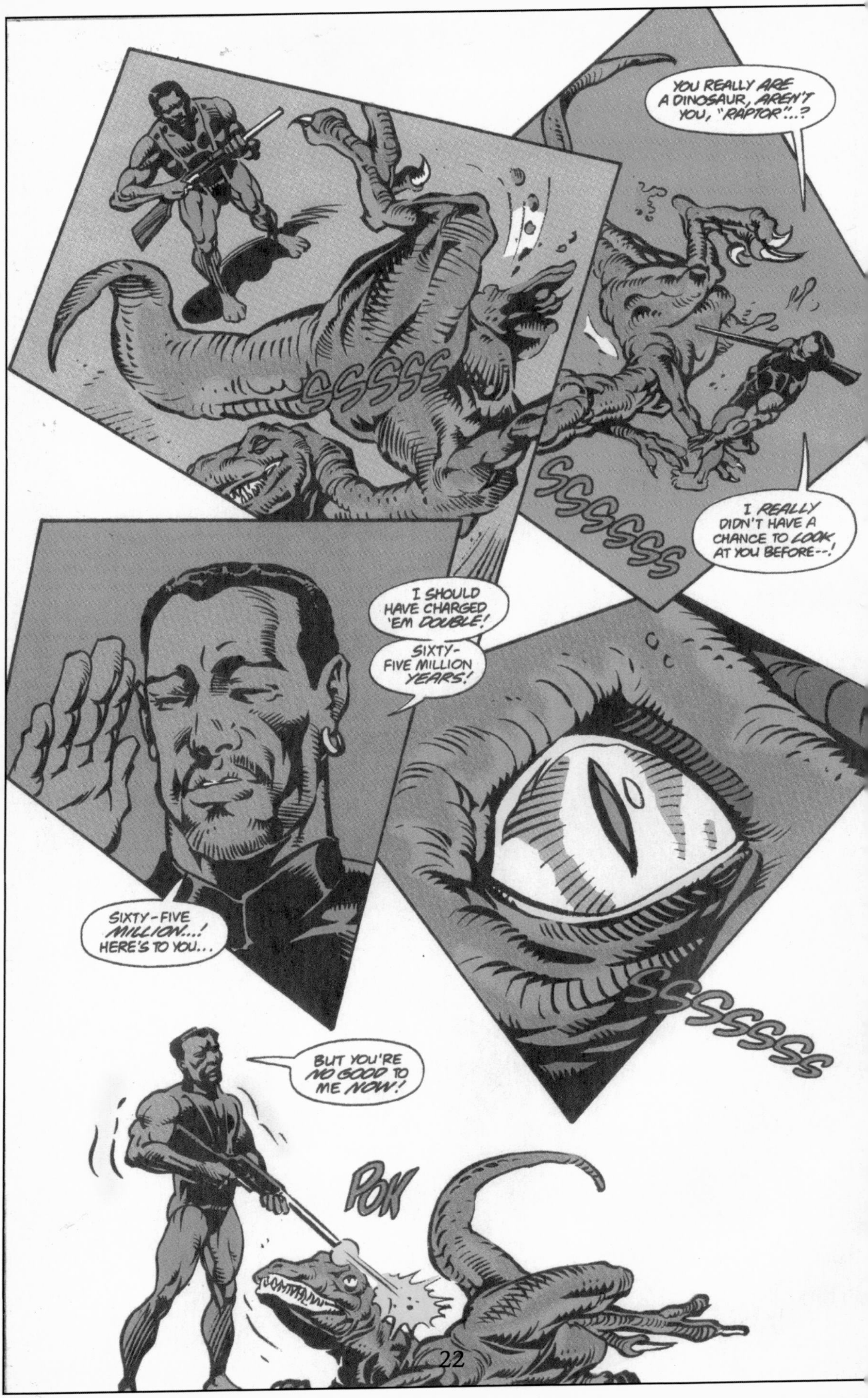
YOU REALLY ARE A DINOSAUR, AREN'T YOU, "RAPTOR"...?
SSSSS
SSSSSS
I REALLY DIDN'T HAVE A CHANCE TO LOOK AT YOU BEFORE--!
I SHOULD HAVE CHARGED 'EM DOUBLE!
SIXTY-FIVE MILLION YEARS!
SIXTY-FIVE MILLION...! HERE'S TO YOU...
SSSSSSS
BUT YOU'RE NO GOOD TO ME NOW!
POK

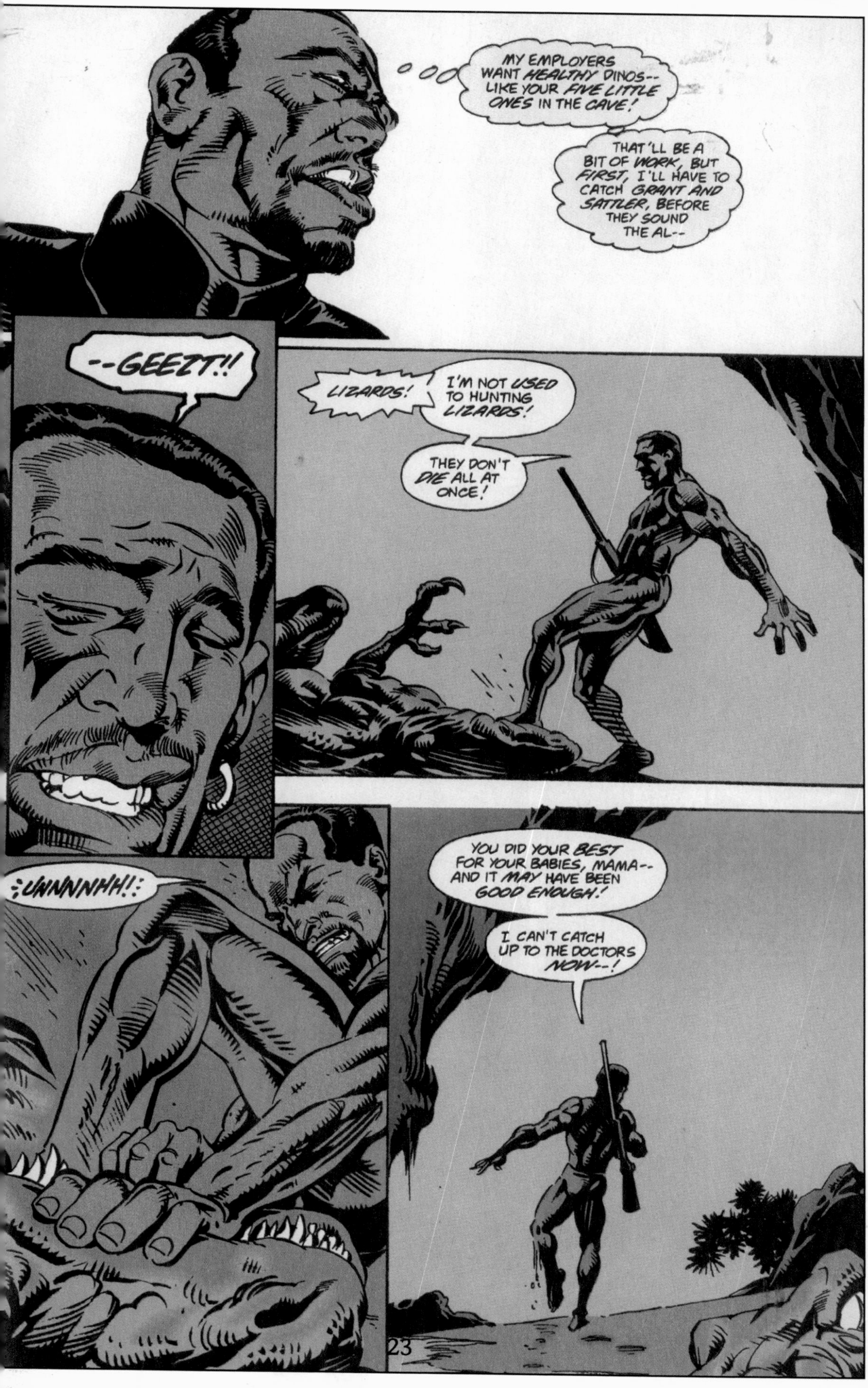
MY EMPLOYERS WANT HEALTHY DINOS-- LIKE YOUR FIVE LITTLE ONES IN THE CAVE!
THAT'LL BE A BIT OF WORK, BUT FIRST, I'LL HAVE TO CATCH GRANT AND SATTLER, BEFORE THEY SOUND THE AL--
--GEEZT!!
LIZARDS!
I'M NOT USED TO HUNTING LIZARDS!
THEY DON'T DIE ALL AT ONCE!
UNNNNHH!
YOU DID YOUR BEST FOR YOUR BABIES, MAMA-- AND IT MAY HAVE BEEN GOOD ENOUGH!
I CAN'T CATCH UP TO THE DOCTORS NOW--!

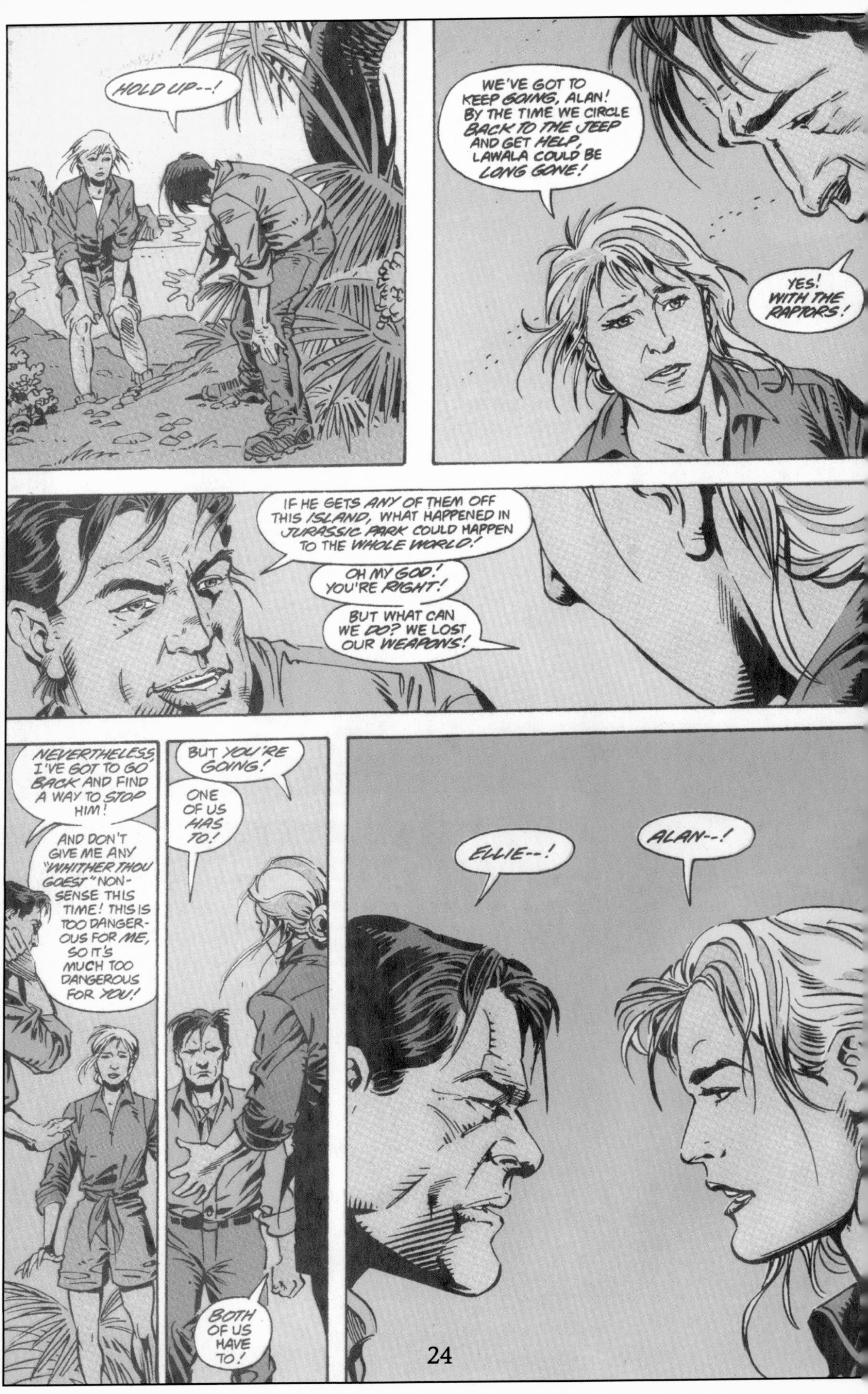
HOLD UP--!
WE'VE GOT TO KEEP GOING, ALAN! BY THE TIME WE CIRCLE BACK TO THE JEEP AND GET HELP, LAWALA COULD BE LONG GONE!
YES! WITH THE RAPTORS!
IF HE GETS ANY OF THEM OFF THIS ISLAND, WHAT HAPPENED IN JURASSIC PARK COULD HAPPEN TO THE WHOLE WORLD!
OH MY GOD! YOU'RE RIGHT!
BUT WHAT CAN WE DO? WE LOST OUR WEAPONS!
NEVERTHELESS, I'VE GOT TO GO BACK AND FIND A WAY TO STOP HIM!
AND DON'T GIVE ME ANY "WHITHER THOU GOEST" NON-SENSE THIS TIME! THIS IS TOO DANGER-OUS FOR ME, SO IT'S MUCH TOO DANGEROUS FOR YOU!
BUT YOU'RE GOING!
ONE OF US HAS TO!
BOTH OF US HAVE TO!
ELLIE--!
ALAN--!

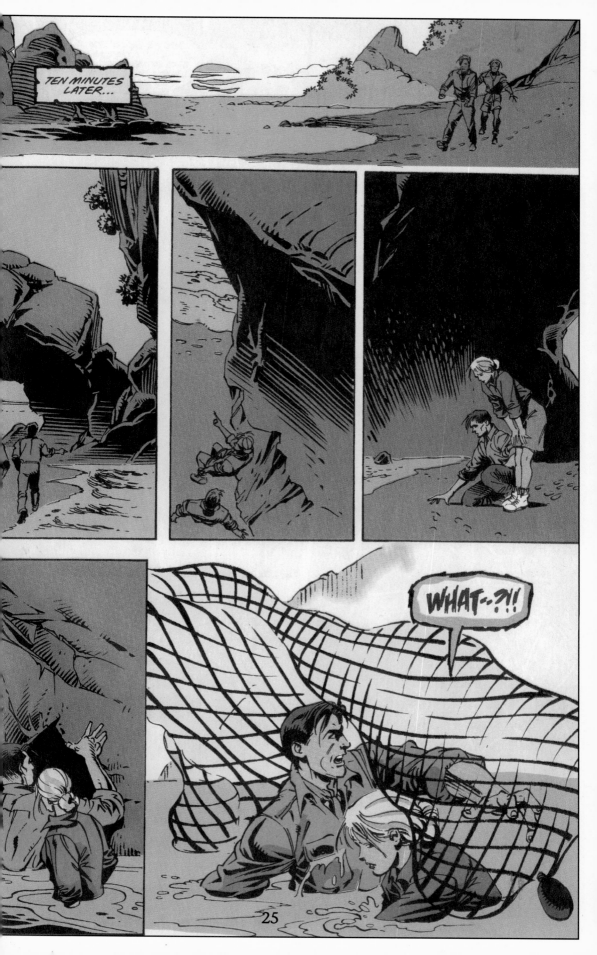

TEN MINUTES LATER...

WHAT--?!!

25

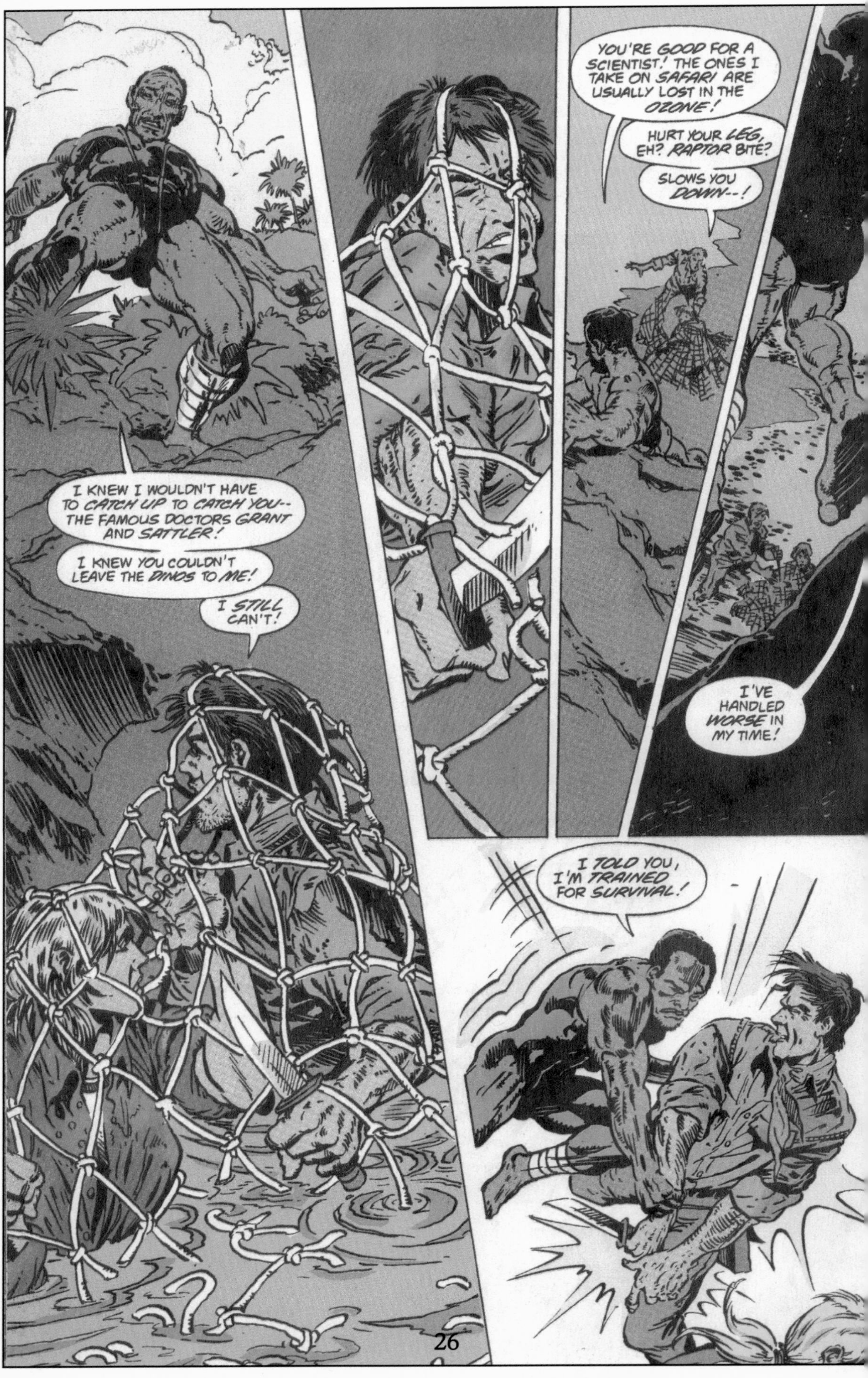
YOU'RE GOOD FOR A SCIENTIST! THE ONES I TAKE ON SAFARI ARE USUALLY LOST IN THE OZONE!
HURT YOUR LEG, EH? RAPTOR BITE?
SLOWS YOU DOWN--!
I'VE HANDLED WORSE IN MY TIME!
I KNEW I WOULDN'T HAVE TO CATCH UP TO CATCH YOU-- THE FAMOUS DOCTORS GRANT AND SATTLER!
I KNEW YOU COULDN'T LEAVE THE DINOS TO ME!
I STILL CAN'T!
I TOLD YOU, I'M TRAINED FOR SURVIVAL!

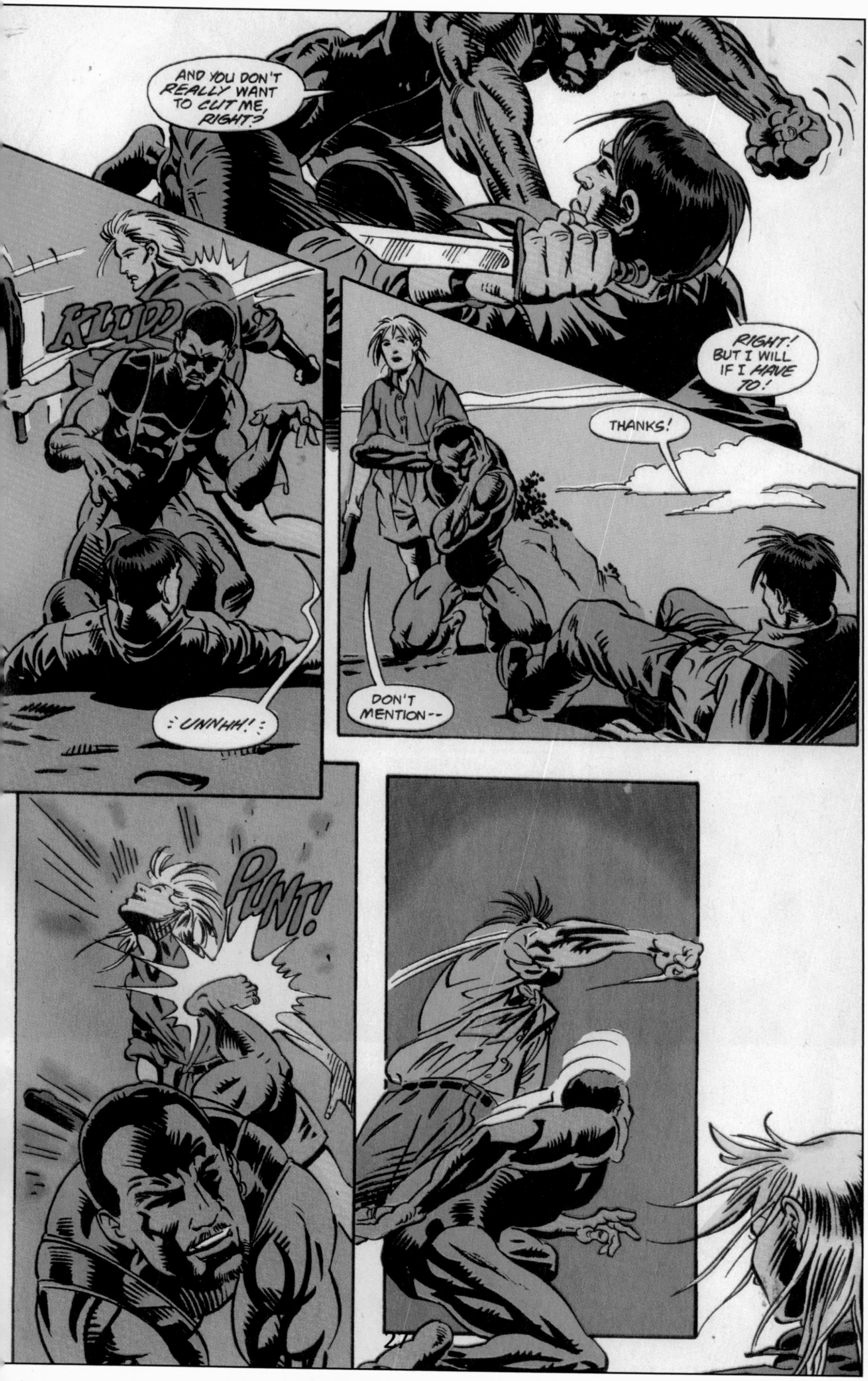
AND YOU DON'T REALLY WANT TO CUT ME, RIGHT?
RIGHT! BUT I WILL IF I HAVE TO!
KLUDD
UNNHH!
THANKS!
DON'T MENTION--
PLUNT!

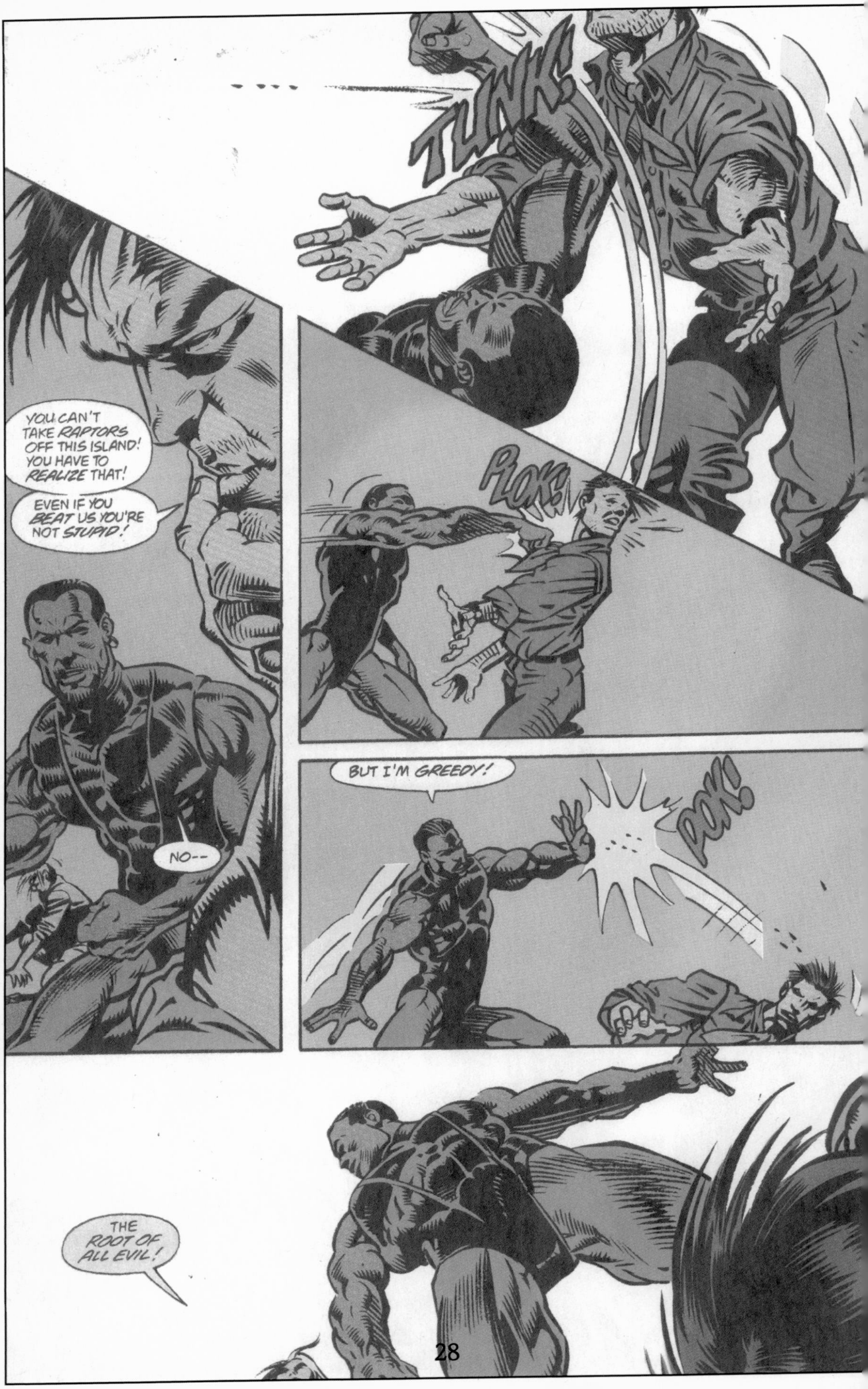
TUNK!
YOU CAN'T TAKE RAPTORS OFF THIS ISLAND! YOU HAVE TO REALIZE THAT!
EVEN IF YOU BEAT US YOU'RE NOT STUPID!
NO--
PLOK!
BUT I'M GREEDY!
POK!
THE ROOT OF ALL EVIL!

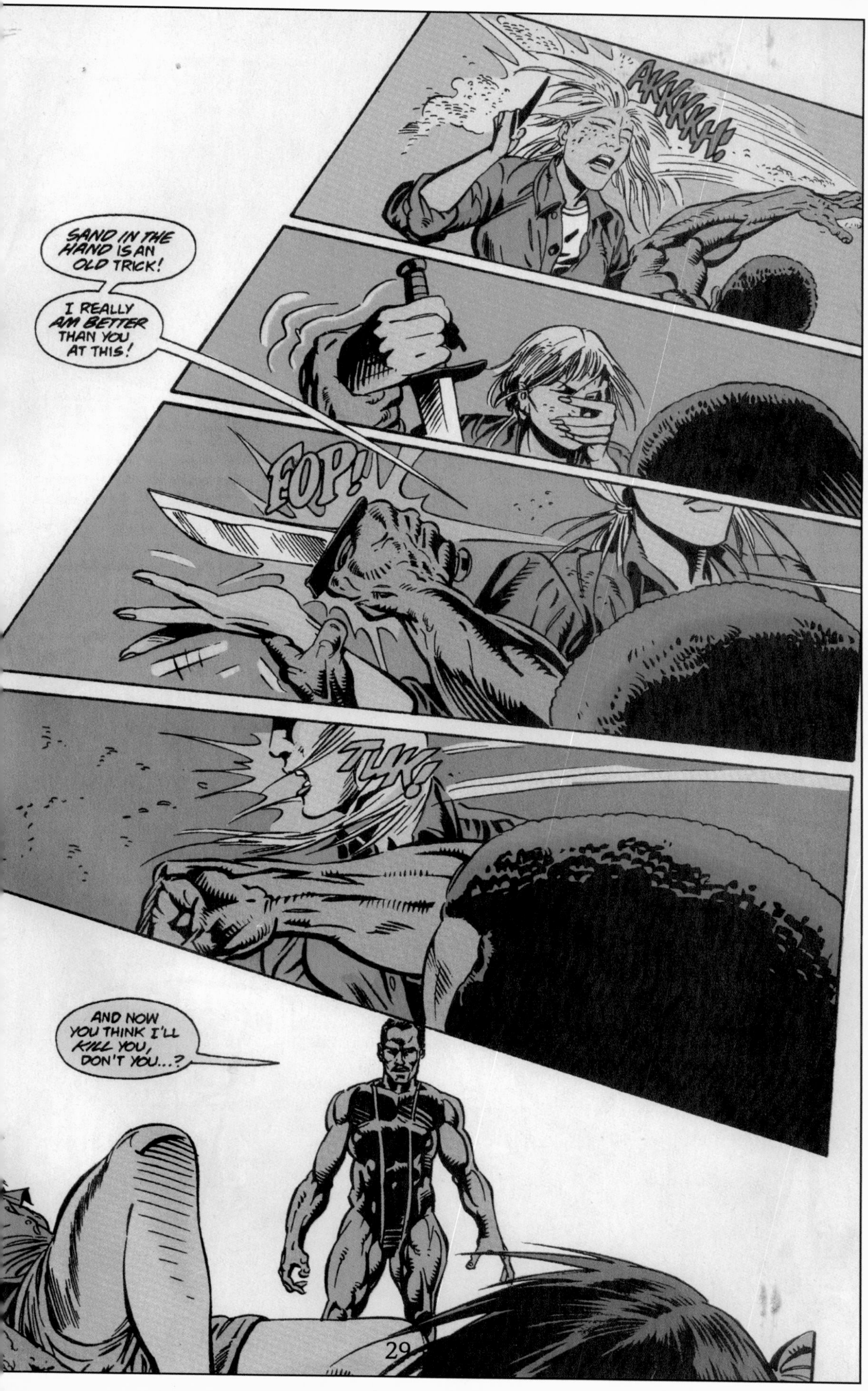
AKKKKH!
SAND IN THE HAND IS AN OLD TRICK!
I REALLY AM BETTER THAN YOU AT THIS!
FOP!
TUK!
AND NOW YOU THINK I'LL KILL YOU, DON'T YOU...?

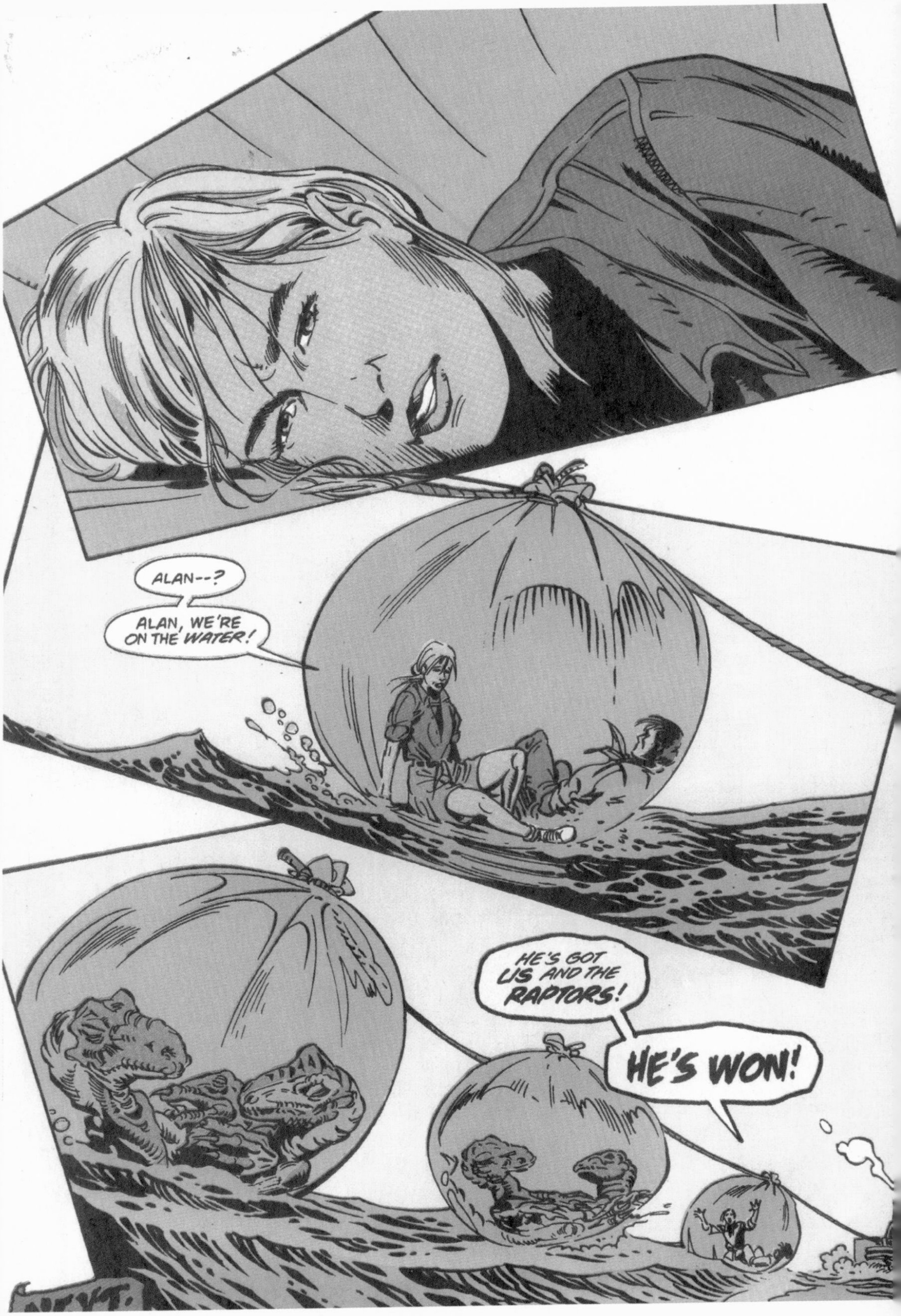
ALAN--?
ALAN, WE'RE ON THE WATER!
HE'S GOT US AND THE RAPTORS!
HE'S WON!